in conversation

by chris campanioni

Agnos Publishing
Honolulu, Hawaii
2014

Published in the USA by Aignos
1910 Ala Moana Blvd, #20A
Honolulu, HI 96815
www.aignos.com

Printed in the USA

Cover art provided by Carlos Alemán
Author Photo by Evelyn Cheung

13-digit ISBN: 978-0-9904322-3-4
10-digit ISBN: 0-9904322-3-8

Aignos Publishing
Honolulu, Hawaii
2014

Also by Chris Campanioni

Going Down
Fashion of the seasons

For Ana,
Who died and breathed life into me

There is nothing unilateral about the human experience. Even solitude has its dialectic. Dialogues exist among and between ourselves, as well as the world we inhabit, and listening requires more than just the faculties of our ears.

My aim is to show the collision and interaction between the lines, like the collision and interaction between our bodies and souls, or between man and technology, or between the street and the subway, or between the past and memory … between time itself. Sometimes even between the words; words that live on in other words; stories that are etched above or faded below other stories; lines that take on new meaning when they bleed across columns and collide.

It is the conversation we need to have.

It is the conversation we are having.

"… in the beginning was the word
The word has been in for a too long time
You in the word and the word in you
We are out
You are in
We have come to let you out."
—Brion Gysin, *Minutes to Go*

table of contents

In Conversation
(the word is yours)

coming
attractions

Coming Attractions

Word games. Rearranged names. A Pepsi ad
administered with pop music; ad nauseam. The smell
of popcorn. Seatbacks shaking. The weight of bodies, expectations; desire

for a payoff or to get what they paid for. People
in pleated jeans and sweatpants and short skirts or shorts,
exposed knees, crossing legs or pressing both feet to the floor, impatient

and/or shaking in between hollow place
holders. Pacing corridors with tremulous steps,
a vast search for a place to rest without a light or sign for

VACANCY. Lights dim. Mouths hymn, hum, shut almost
completely as the projector clicks and the reel moves,
a shudder at the gate. The image slides, rising like a shadow from above.

A baby cries.

A memory of middle school

tube tops shimmering on the darkened
stage—a gym—half-decorated
in shades of black and gold,
banners, posters, unrolled ribbons,
prone confetti, the other half
still baring the unlit scoreboard
blaring last night's game. We lost.

I slide, or rather slip, or rather fall
unwittingly into another's arms,
bump and grind and agonized
by a motive midriff
(sex as motif if I ever read one)—
what crossed my eyes?

Another love? Another guise? A memory
from the solvent well of childhood
returning to my writer's mind.

Imagine something as something else.
Picture a carpet, a room with a view,
a desk, a wooden chair, open
notebook, uncapped pen
(two more nearby, as a rule)
crossing out and underlining, reframing

a memory of middle school

Inheritance

I am the speaker in the poem.
I call attention to the meaning
of form, informed by my ancestry,
not just lines but their lineage;
substance as source.
I don't want to hide behind
language—body
or otherwise—and besides,
it all comes back as intercourse.

I want to lay it on the table—
no that's not right—
I want to lay it on,
simple and concise,
I want to lay with you and melt
right in, oozing with spermicide
and the milk of human kindness
like Ishmael would have liked, even
like Modern English:
I'll stop the world
and melt with you
I want to paint the walls read
from the Sanskrit rādhnoti.
I want to confuse my verbs and my adjectives
until they become indistinguishable.

I pledge allegiance
to movement, to rhythm,
to words interacting
with words, word
play, the play within
the play: All the words
a stage and most of all, poetry.

I feel the same things Sophocles
on a darkling plain felt, differently.
I want to ascertain the whole range
of human understanding, lost
or longing by definition,
necessary yearning.

Call me languished
from languor, from the Latin languēre.
See also: fade, waste, wilt, wither, go,
as in to move, or proceed, especially
to or from something.
See also: volta,
a turn, from the Latin
verso. No resolution
as resonant as a shift
in tone or mood. Haven't you
ever heard from your
mother-father-daughter-sister
It's not what you said, it's how you said it?
I forgot the sun,
too, the way sometimes glare
obscures the truth.

And the you that I am invoking is not you
but me, the you that I am
invoking isn't the reader
Whitman would have loved to meet
months or years later,
just me, the way *you*
sometimes ask yourself
God, what have you done?
and forget you are looking inwardly.
Language is a tricky thing.

My mother speaks in contradictions.

She says Yeah, followed by No
when she really means, Yes, sometimes, even
Certainly. In the act of creation,
as in all the arts,
the soul should be felt
in the face and the fingers
and the tongue, even
in the cavities,
from the Latin cavo
and cavare: to excavate.

People live on in other people's memories.
I read that looking at old photographs
is another form of time-travel.
My mother's childhood
is also her child's.

Play This Back

To feel her is to be underwater, speaking
in bubbles and watching the sea life slip
past your eyes like captions for the hearing

impaired, the rush and ripple of waves tickling
your hairs, each follicle, every split in the skin
breaking and receding, or to be under a water-

fall, gusts of cold shock coming uninterrupted
and with pebble interjections from time
to time, arms up, raised high in eternal

ecstasy of a single moment, or to fly,
gliding through clouds and the ozone
or Interzone or the intervals

of the commute, customs after airport security,
a snake undulating in the grooves between
bodies, between spaces, between the spaces

between space, or to ride, in the passenger seat
or simply as a passenger, head-hanging out
the half-held sliding translucence

with the illusory blue line on the left, right,
and above all else, above: invisible stitching
of the sky or simply the continuous sea

wall, a reflection or refraction or induction
deduced by binoculars miles and miles and miles
away from shore unless it's a block away

and you're driving through the boardwalk,

or a billboard of the same thing passing
and all of life is illusion anyway except feeling,

which is what I set out to say, or to speak, specks
of language, expressions ebbing and departing before
I can pinpoint the details, exact specifications

and dimensions of the way she feels or the way
I feel when I'm inside her and she inside me,
turning inward as two shells cupped to each ear:

the roar of the past (a distant memory), each
fleeting moment between here and there—
a sensation heightened if I'm listening

to a particular song at a particular moment
when I play *this* back on memory, by which
I mean my mind's eye: always set to record

and never fully paused for anything other than
scribbles, sentence-fragments, a mass
of letters, trying to recall enough to

play it back at some other time,
afraid to finally stop, afraid to come
to the end, to say good-bye, to call it

quits with a hard return and a period, too.

Play this back
to the end, to say good-bye, to call me
afraid, to finally stop, afraid to come.

Play it back at some other time
with letters, trying to recall enough to
scribble sentence-fragments amassed

and never fully pause for anything other than—
I mean my mind's eye: always set to record
when I play *this* back on memory, by which

a particular song at a particular moment,
a sensation heightened if I'm listening
to fleeting moments between here and there

the roar of the past (a distant memory), us
turning inward as two shells cupped to each ear.
I feel when I'm inside her and she inside me,

and dimensions of the way she feels or the way
I can pinpoint the details, exact specifications
of language, expressions ebbing and departing before

which is what I set out to say, or to speak, specks
and all of life is illusion anyway except feeling,
or a billboard of the same thing passing

and you're driving through the boardwalk,
away from shore unless it's a block away
deduced by binoculars miles and miles and miles

of wall, a reflection or refraction or induction
of the sky or simply the continuous sea
and above all else, above invisible stitching

with the illusory blue line on the left, right,
the half-held sliding translucence
or simply as a passenger, head-hanging out

between space, or to ride in the passenger seat.
Bodies between spaces, between the spaces:
a snake undulating in the grooves between

the commute, customs after airport security,
or Interzone or the intervals
gliding through clouds and the ozone

ecstasy of a single moment, or to fly
to time, arms up, raised high in eternal
pebble interjections from time-

fall, gusts of cold shock coming uninterrupted,
breaking and receding, or to be under
your hairs, each follicle, every split in the skin

impaired, the rush and ripple of waves tickling
past your eyes like captions for the hearing
in bubbles and watching the sea life slip.

To feel her is to be underwater, speaking.

Ars Poetica

She pulled up in a white Lexus.
She's taking me for a ride.
No, really, it's more
than simply expression. Promises
always produce possibilities.
I am a passenger.

This is a poem.

I refuse to write in abstractions,
antique language, indistinct symbols.
Poetry is never about climbing mountains
unless there are mountains and someone climbing one
or a multitude of peaks.
Slow down, or simply
take it easy.
We might have built pretty rooms
with pithy sonnets
but just because I drew
a rainbow doesn't mean
I proved its covenant.

Growing Up, Getting Slack

You saw the chase
from another side of the side
walk, across the street, twenty
floors up, between
the ampersand of white

washed walls and every
day demands, quarterly
finance reports, analysis; quarters,
nickels, dimes, most of all
dollars. Analytically dying.

Both feet in quick
sand. You thought
of childhood, you thought of man
hunt, or hide
and seek, waiting

in the woods twenty
years before, wouldn't be more
than an hour …
you were nickel and dimed.
What are you hiding from now?

Among the hurry and the crowd
of heads down, swinging brief
cases or backpacks, backs
bent low, unsmiling,
untiring, slow and steady

or fast and ready
at a moment's notice,
briefly cognizant,

and the click-a-clack
of heels on tiled floor,

scurrying for the ten
trials of Hercules.
Here's one more
to fill the bric-a-brac.
Here's one more

to make the still sun run.
"Marvelous, darling"
she purred, furnishing
another false embrace.
You thought of daring

gun chases you
worshipped on TV
growing up and getting slack,
and going down
the street is really

just a foot race
between two children
in matching slacks
and shoes, playing hooky
this afternoon.

Nominative Absolute

Death is in the restroom
staring at my reflection
in the mirror.

I see myself in the future
tense, imperfect past,
or simply participle

(present only
in pieces).
Such a night.

In my bed, I watch people
on the screen, and hear
the clock tick—

cricket, cricket—
patient fakings,
a boom mic

hanging between the cracks
of luminescence. Such a night
for something to feel so

exact and at the same time
lacking. Absent.
Such a night.

This is best read
in the time it takes to play
the musical companion.

(New Order: Age of Consent)

Death is in the kitchen sink,
and I am washing my hands
of him.

I would have told you

in my father's house there are many
mansions. I remember the passion
of adolescence, bodies
of water, rhythmic slapping
during rain, before/after, over
hill and dale and lake,
panting rush of skin.

Let me start again. I ran
that sentence into the ground so
to speak. Speak loudly,
and never be afraid
to go out on a limb—
my mother's words, my father's—
Man's sins, there are many, many ...

a paper flower dropped in a cup of water
succored with yellow petals
glistened with spit.

Ciphers

i.
Sweat on steel marks the day, nightfall comes,
the scythe remains, a hint of sullen silver
suddenly arcs, and bends, and breaks—departs.

He is marked by the soil, the dark patches
blur his face, a matchstick used, returned again
each morning, every day; the boils on his toes
are always, and endless, like the rows of wheat

and grain he reaps, meeting no voice
to listen, or to speak, no face revealed
but the face that stares back
placid on steel.

ii.
Back bent low, tired,
unsmiling. Slow
drips of sweat
from brow to lino
(unmopped for now,

viscid and moist).
Child's cries answered
in some coarse voice;
of course she's tired—
it's 3 a.m. again,

and the reflection
from panes shows pain
in her eyes, big, brown,
bloodshot
in the dim light.

iii.
He slides in at the booth at *Sam's*,
orders a drink and runs his hand
through tousled hair. He waits
for his lover there: a leathered

briefcase with initials
slapped across the side, where he chides
himself once or twice before subsiding
to lust, ravishes the papers,

consumes the ink while others
around him act merry and think,
"Who goes to a bar to do work?"
with confused whispers and toxic smirks.

iv.
Now wait, now watch, now pass
the time, and wonder how long
this will last, or wonder
where they pick the songs
that play now, from secret
unseen stereos.

I know this couch—
discolored, and somewhere
between retro and the art deco
adorning walls, in ways
that aren't in, in ways
that haven't been

fashionable and will never be—
sees many visitors
(just echoes).
Sees everyday

a new story, a new trace
of human misery.

We seep in,
creeping slowly
to these polyester
arms, ragged worn and thin,
alarmed at our promiscuity
when we move on,

moments later; disarmed
and ever lonely.

This place is electric

These faces, the sounds, each spry hop
back to the coarse dirt mound—
Who's on first? The thirst
of a thousand people capitulates here

where some dreams go to die
and others, more fortunate, survive
a boundless fate—this is not
just a game. I came too.
Countless maxims remind me each moment I've forgot

that this place has been born and died,
and again, begot,
no sense of dread collective
as our sense of death,
or, in living, this place to seem

unseemly, with perpetual lament.
No sport of His neglects the day
you die, where there is only one out
and no dropped fly balls
anybody will ever recall.

On the corner of a sprawling southern city

nearby the old ONI and US Postal
building where peddlers spit
crab shells and Creole ditties,
both doors remain boarded.
Scattered papers and sordid lies
survive the office at 544 Camp Street
in which men in black suits and matching
ties would meet, clandestine, huddled
in smoke filled rooms, maracas
playing somewhere, talks of soft
politics and military coups
in the humid Louisianan air
where on certain nights a languid breeze
leaves traces of the foul stench
still lingering to kill a king.

Nervous in the Service

Shades on to keep the shine out,
mumbling whispers, shouts and bullet kisses,
foreign tongues spit fast in the desert sun.
Explosions bounce
two feet left,
        five feet right,
                now in front,
        now in back,
a tango in the sand, dancing
between cacti with sirens blaring creating
crescendo of thoughts and daring leaps from present
to past and back again; a different world here,
no place for boys with dreams, jump to the corner
of 40th and Maine, dollar apple pies and ice cream
sandwiches, stragglers on the corner pushing tin cans
"I'm between careers."

Time slows, sound dulls to ear,
barrel recoils splitting flesh from the seams,
metal casings spraying, dust and hips
swaying, saying
softly, a thought forms on his lips—
Nervous in the service

Headlines

Clay walls, final curtain calls—no
time or need to take a bow—
paved courtyard entrenched

in desert, secret, seemingly
deserted, all around
the sound of whispers like a prayer

and over there: a center
of learning, or a cell,
what the TV calls it, a few

thousand yells and screams on screen dissolve
into just one
headline the next morning.

Far away now, somewhere
more modern, more
urban (hard to believe

only distance separates
the two): He yawns,
blue bathrobe on,

swallowing the news
with an English muffin and jam:
TERRORISTS STRIKE THE CAPITAL

AGAIN—It's suicide
prescribed. As the jelly
falls on his knees,

the pale flesh
etched in braille red ink,
he sighs.

Gunshot. A few more

cracks of smoke across the drag
of lonely sand, expanded by the quiet
and the day, the bright glare, the rust
and decay of an ancient city that belongs
to no one now, and is nowhere
but here. He has no fear

within these forlorn walls, learned
to refuse it from the whistles and roll
calls, the cracking wind and cold command—
demands of a Marine undreaming. The man,
meanwhile, hunched atop the roof, scuttles
and moves between the rubble of rough
clay beneath boots. The bullets
brush dust from the soil, one pupil
shuts, the steel recoils after each round
expands and moves, expels.

No one else will be alive to tell
what happens next—understand,
back when I knew him, he was shy
and less brave than he is now:
Crowded among the smears of red and beige
and black of dusk that tempers us and puts
our thoughts to bed, his body
leaves a book of dreams that dissipates
and then returns, unread.

Walk, Trot, Canter, Gallop

When they took her she didn't scream.
Between the old Victrola
playing in papa's study
and the whispers of some forgotten
dream, she was only confused.

Now she stood accused of nothing
and already bounded in a train:
crowded, headed east;
feet sockless numb, face bruised
from the force of the blunt stick struck

against flesh when she sobbed
at last, her papa lying in a heap
as a shadow pressed against the panes
of cold wood and sullen thoughts,
and a fading Krakowiak tune

she never lost. She was
twelve in 1942.

June 1968

Aquí de "hacero" con mi rifle automático M-16 Tira 20 tiros en 2½ segundos, pesa solo 7½ cargado. Tira tiro a tiro también

You wrote, "hachero"
Loosely translated:
Bon vivant
Cool guy

You're dramatic by design,

poised and ready like a G.I. Joe
molded out of mud and soil—
the roar and recoil
of basic training—
cigarette dangling
deftly from your lips
I know you
never smoked. You're soaked
in California sweat
and green as an adolescent
in a strange land, the spire oaks
draped in the back
ground, the pants and shirt and helmet
covering your brow, everything
bathed in camo.

Back-and-forth, falling
into order as the clouds crease
into evening, hardly a moment
to breathe between jumping-
jacks and harsh commands,
the whole company shouting
separately at the same time,
visions of winnows
seething through so many
attentive eyes,
empiric windowsills, and still
you have the same half-smile I've imitated
for the past twenty years, the familiar details
I inherited and which every day I will see
in the mirror, scrutinize.
As the breeze picks up from the Pacific,
you see the future you will make
in this new country, staring through fear and morning.

You sleep in flits, restive and resistant,
and the only father you
invoked that day is the Father to whom you prayed,

the Father that allowed you to have a family, farther
from the collapse of faith,
murder masquerading as democracy
"And ring from all the trees" or
"The twilight's last gleaming" below
the swath of colors in the sky before a storm,
split-level sleeping
quarters, top and bottom bunks with no room
for comfort, much less botany.
You found instead:

Life, liberty, the pursuit of
everything. Thumbs-up instead of coup d'états,
a Polish girl with kind green eyes
and pale, raised cheeks. *Zosia.*
Language barriers. Boundless streets.
Fatherhood. Pizza and Ovaltine,
and the endless rows of puffed wheat,
General Mills or Kellogg's, cereal sweeter
than sugar cubes; unnatural, reduced to additives.
Too much, never enough
variety. Unsettling
as icicles. They didn't have those in Cuba.

Dearest Beloved,
(after Astrophil)

I dub myself incompetent,
inclined to modesty and incapable
of loving moderately; hence
my proposal, a bouquet

of promises the most promiscuous
shepherd could never make
to his or her coy mistress, marvel at this:
I want to resuscitate

all the curse words that were cast out
of every English-speaking class
from Elizabethan England to devout
Pilgrim settlers and unsettle you with crass

attitudes and inappropriate anachronisms.
I want to write palinodes in terza rima
imbued with meaningful Malapropisms,
which is to say nothing about sonnets and stiff rimes.

(I'm not Donne yet.)

I want to live in Dickens' city.
I want to have a country wife.
We were not born with two feet
to move through paradise alone. I've tried

to write a poem to abate a vacancy,
though I suppose I'm only writing to say, "you please me."

Hoodwinked in Hackensack

All the people I love came here.
Babcia, Abuela, Ciocia Jadzia, Aunt Nena, all the kids
from St. Mary's Pre-K convening for an evening of Fun
Time Pizza, piñata, arcade games, skeet ball, ice cream
in miniature plastic caps and piña coladas—too many,

too sweet—with toothpicked umbrellas
for the grownups slumped in seats
or slurring their speech
patterns of genealogy.
Sto lat, sto lat, niech żyje, żyje nam and more

words I can sing but can't understand;
I mimic my mother. I wonder
when I can open my first gift, sifting through ribbons
and carefully-wrapped rectangles, shaking each *regalo*
as the sound increases from animals, a band

of characters dressed in blue and pink
garments, gowns and suits, instruments affixed
to their arms, a tuba, a tambourine, a mic in hand
clanging in the distance until the routine ends.
All the people I love can't hear

my questions, incessant declarations of a five-year-old—
five-and-a-few-hours I remind Dad—as of two today.
¡Dale, dale! Tribilín but then I'm led by the hand
unwillingly. *Can you keep a secret?*
My brother slips past the velvet

to show me the mannequins, inanimate,
limbs without life, withdrawn.
What's wrong with them?
I ask, aghast, but he's gone and I'm alone,
clambering out from the curtains

into a sea of faces, waves, tidings,

a camcorder recording it all.
I flinch, squint
into so many tears.
All the people I love disappeared.

Graduation

Face down lying
on a cot—twin-sized and characterized
by not so subtle knots
and stains (blame love

making or make your own
excuse), I lose myself
in a haze of memories
that might be unremembered

by anyone but me. I think
it's pertinent to peruse
the last four years
like they were bric-a-brac

attached to some antique
store, paved brick entrance
to my mind, scoured for posterity
or simply consigned

to consumption; fast, easy,
like candy at a cinema
concession stand.
And where do I go from here?

I fear the uncertain, the change
dangling from pockets of time like oranges
in grove, the thought of years
passing years until age becomes

imperceptible, the face
in my father's medicine
cabinet mirror is not mine

yet. Let's go,

and not forget what got us here
in the first place, huddled
between a world of born
and a world of made, and swarm

the arching causeways
of causality; I never thought
in West New York, shaking
on my seat, Dad's outstretched

arms trying to guide me
on the four-wheeler
(I never graduated to a bike)
would ever see the day

I'd graduate
from a child
to something like a man.
It's only me,

spin that fast
and anything becomes
unlasting. *It's dangerous,
slow down* and all around

the impermanent glaze
of movement: My father's
concerned gaze at my back,
my lack of bewilderment.

Have Psychoanalytical Theory, Will Travel

In the haze of June burning
through July, of the opaque
churning of time wasting
time, I awoke bored,
became morose,

longed for more adventure,
to do anything worth remembering.
As if I could just find life
in my lap like some tattered
coffee-stained treasure map,

as if I could be alive
at my leisure, never mind
that. My mother's tan Volvo
wagon had a knack for breaking down
on the road as I broke state boundaries,

bound by the speed limit
but hardly anything else;
self-discovery via recurrent radio waves,
blaring in and out
of focus, scattered on a stretch

of road like a million swarming locusts—
the ten plagues
of July from an unlit,
open sky. I counted time
in mileage, days crossed off

an imaginary calendar like target practice,
one by one, gone
to the gallows. I passed

the loneliest stretch of highway
in the world, hitchhiker's holding signs—

HAVE PSYCHOANALYTICAL THEORY,
WILL TRAVEL—signs
of the times, faces melted
in a puddle of sun on asphalt;
the fault of the economy,

or blame it on booze.
I roared across a million
different glamour stores
all selling the same thing—
advertisements inked with a gleam

of hope in reality's despair—
and thought of the soap
my aunt used to watch,
air waves signaling back
our dreams, what we're meant to believe,

the whole while unbelieving
any of it could ever possibly
be real.
I ate time, chewed
it lewd and greedy.

I wanted more of it,
tortured lurid
among the scores
of billboards and bric-a-brac
attached at the hip of freeway,

someone's unwanted gifts
discarded and forgot.
I thought of Columbus

and Cortés, and all the other names
our history says is important.

I counted myself more fortunate
than the majestic beasts that roamed
these streets at some time, before
there were streets, before
almost anything worthwhile.

Never mind
those books of history
Ötzi the Iceman couldn't read,
it still happened;
he was there.

Disclosures

"I have an affinity for Orientals."
We were talking about carpets
in relation to my bedroom,
particularly the interior decoration,
whether lino was inferior to wooden tile;
I nearly fell asleep before she paused
to swallow.

Let's Go

Last night's dream:
A tango to the "Ride of the Valkyries"
(yeah, right), rendezvous
via starlight, calm Dover
evening—open sky, seeming

to be at once a memory
and a moment of someone
else's life at the same time—
Hollywood's version instead.
You led me by the hand, vaulted

past some vast and trackless
stretch of sand (eighteenth-century
brick road just moments before), a purse
of Shelley. You were
speaking to me, sleeveless

shirt and jeans rolled up
to my knees—Levi's, and T.S.
Eliot's idea of a beach
wanderer wondering where
all the world has gone—all

the clamor, the hurry, the pace,
all the people speaking like speakeasies
in Prohibition's spectral embrace—
quiet, remote, clouds of 1927
smoke from an alleyway three

knocks at a time, clandestine. Always
like that, communication in a cloth
of signs, muted by messages, imbibed

and spat back, returned to sender, end
to end, a whole lifespan convinced of Hell

if I know. Let's go.
Ephemeral. Let time
dissolve and let's time travel, let's escape
like some escapist's fantasy, some pleasure
seeker fancying more, mourning what

we can't have. Nothing
lasts. On the corner
of consciousness and waking
avenue you leave me, disarmed, fleeting
to the beep of a desk lamp alarm.

The Lover (our hero)

wakes in the morning,
yawning angel by his side
(the *Hero* is grizzly masculine
and calm as a mannequin
at a department store, men's
fashion side). He finds

the *Student* in the afternoon
reading Derrida and Einstein's theory
of relativity in a restless classroom,
greets the *Athlete*
at 4, glazed sweat
gleaming in the steel
reflection of weights

(his garlic breath
from the hors d'oeuvres
the *Cook* made hours
before) and leaves,
as the *Adulterer*
graces his fling
in Wrigley's spearmint

and dark jeans in evening.
I am all of these, mixed
colors with whites
and made the laundry malfunction.
I see from two eyes as a type
of personas, playbill
at theater, theatrical

production, buried
like a masterpiece

dug up years or moments
later, like Rossetti's long
deceased wife, a rose
for Emily. Bouquet
of flowers, a thousand

vibrant dandelions, sight
for sore eyes exploding
in her face—my
mother's—her garden
was never made
for just the décor.

The Signifier and the Signified

The erratic crack of love
on flesh enmeshes
with his thoughtfulness—he thinks
during climax, eyes peeled
slowly back,
legs

      rapture
arms

      arms
wrapping legs—which comes first?

In the slaking flood and sludge of sound,
there are only ideas. He fears
he can only ever be ideas—
the semblance of a boy—
when he was in elementary school,
he played imaginary games, all the while,
he thought growing up never came
until it comes in the notion
of a teenager, somebody's virulent son,
excited by the conceit

of living free; uninhibited, sporadic.
He spasms at the reaction of love
making orgasm and vice
versa, curls his tongue
over some delicate words,
designates his diction
as finite. Finally
a turn, a bend and lean
to realize the seams unsewn
in his mind—not right, just

almost, not quite. Never
in all the glare of truth,
of an unreachable place of solitude
could he ever identify
the signified from the sign,
the postcard of an Aztec temple
inscribed in Kodak
furnished on a wall,
or the lush Austrian countryside, cowbells
and singing nuns; photographs
re-presenting representations
of imagined lives. His-
tory lies dormant, lives
in monuments
for all the world to see.

He is presented
with the past, freeze frames,
space blurs, outside his head
and inside her. Alarming
acknowledgements ferment the sweat
uncovered in sin, just an idea
of love, just his concept.

Evening in Autumn

We watched the moon soar
above the clouds, and swore
off all the crowds that gathered
at the movies, or loud bars,
or the pretty please flash dance
pageantries, or the backseats
of cars. We were far
too attached at the hip
and content to simply slip
from the stars to each
other's arms in secret, unwatched
to watch the sky, perched
on some parking lot curbside,
shirt off to let you sit dry. Still

the morning came in high
pitched blares and motor
drones to take our peace
away; alone and melancholy
again, and the fires
of last night's piecemeal
flight to Paradise
in pieces, a memory.

Origins

In a well-lit room, in a bank
two blocks from the 4,5 train
on floor 22, with a view
permitting the plaza on Pine,
seen at morning, or evening,
in autumn, or spring, winter
even, certainly in summer,
two people pass each other
(at the lunch room? at the water cooler?
in meetings and mistaken directions, dimensions—
north by northwest—prearranged finance reports,
daily, once or twice; how many
times?), shrewd glances from two
desks separated by

six feet and chance.
A dark-haired Cuban with a cowlick grin.
A Polish girl with kind green eyes
and pale, raised cheeks. Suggestions.
Juan and Zosia. They converged
in a sprawling New York City
and found life, liberty, the pursuit of
everything. Language
barriers. Boundless streets.
As is so seldom the case
between strangers
who might meet, who might fall in love,
as is so seldom the case,
two people embrace.

Making an Exit

i.
Evening. Summer
in Seaside, *Great place*
for the family to stop!
on a sign. Leaves brush, rustle
past a parking lot
toward a vacant curbside
where sleeveless vagrants
might wrestle
with fate. Wind splinters
sand, a sieve
in the wood. Cut
to the dance,
the lithe romance
of moon to sky. Pale
light to earth marks
the boardwalk where he sits
bored, eyes glazed unconcerned
(he's drunk). Still
the darkness
comes, the infinity,
the vast expanse
of what?

He doesn't know
and wishes
he'd never asked. He relapses
into a state of sober disbelief
(Are we really that small?)
where all around is the same
image, same odor—nothing-
ness, just space, lonely
lights in between,

at times seeming to decorate
the black like shapes that coalesce
on fine china plates. It is Dancing

with the Stars sans the strobe
lights and designer
wear and he, of course, is standing
still, petrified, finally aware
of the constellations far
and away, a lovely scene
M.C. Escher or Monet
may have painted
some time or not,
no matter: Everything
has an exit—just not
the sky.

ii.
Flowers line the courtyard
near the entrance—all colors,
all kinds, dandelions
and chrysanthemums circumscribed
for passersby, reminders
of fate, call it destiny
call it whatever you'd like.
We all die. Funny
with the school nearby,
cemetery and a center of learning
and next on the bus tour
is the land of make-believe,
death in slow motion, lively sign
pointing THIS WAY
to Kirkland Village.

iii.
Today he's blue—

not quite
melancholy, just dressed
                        in it, blue jeans,
T-shirt tucked
            at the hip
and it spells, "Hi,
                I'm confused."
He sits amused,
                name tag reads "Fred"
a red scrawl of ink
                        on a sticker
sheet pinned
            to his breast.
What is it
            that keeps shining
in his eyes?
                Shimmer of soul,
kindred spirit
            who wakes
every Friday from
                ten to eleven then ends,
return to sender
                and back again next week,
conflict of interest.
                I can do this, I can
do this, he must think,
                    unthinking.
Resident self-determination
                    is what the guidebook calls it.

iv.
Enter class, backpacks
and claps of hands to back
(concentric circles
and other secrets
of the trade) and made

up smiles and heightened
voices like conversation
with babies or domesticated
animals, just infant noise.
We will not all make

great pets
one student thinks and sinks
into regret for forgetting
to remember that here
is the land of make
believe and neglect. *"Do you
remember me?"* But see—
in fact, Fred nods.

It's all ritual now, greeting
and a warm smile and *"hey,
how are you?"* as if they've
known each other for a while—
they haven't—but that's besides
the point. It's story time.

Baby and a bear, milk bottle
laced with cyanide—suppressed
memories or comedy confided
in a room of strangers
with threads that grow stranger,
and lots of laughter, eyes
that glow for minutes
at a time—wonderful
success, we could say
if we all just forgot
about the bad days: *"Are you
my father?"* Some other time
he wouldn't be, would be
student, twenty-two,

approaching graduate
of the Arts & Sciences
but oh, there are identity crises
and there are aliases
to be made. But see—
in fact, he nods.

v.
A whole life in numbers.
Every 72 seconds someone in America is diagnosed with Alzheimer's.
32.8 percent change in death rate from 2000 to 2004.
Four years of death begets four more,
rising from fifty thousand to sixty-six,
California, Florida and Texas,
the big three
in state-by-state prevalence,
all dead.

And where's the evidence?
These are pieces
to a mystery
not meant to be solved

and at the same time, relentless.
The grief, the deaths, the questions,
too vast to count too fast to cope—
but that is how we go.
Suddenly, and without warning.

vi.
And this is it, the end,
listening to some Stills
song on my lap
top, air as still
as—well, air, not
the most clever analogy

but concise. Wouldn't it be
nice to know
what happens next?
I'm talking post
graduation. This is always
the case. The end
is always only the start
of something else, or else
it's the end, total and absolute,
a salute to mortality, farewell
to arms, disarmed and reticent,
this is it, no more.

That boy before was me,
languishing in the Seaside wind
and wondering why
the universe has to be so permanent, so vast,
flesh and thoughts unlasting.

These thoughts won't last,
not when I'm old
enough to forget
the thoughts inside my head,
led unaided down the corridor
of fantasy and see—
how better it might be to be naïve.
Consciousness could be a curse
but even Hardy would conceive
it worse to lose his own
identity. I think.

That's me
in the mirror,
tanned and hair styled
just the way I like,
hazel eyes and blond

brown hair—and where
will it end? Pretend
that face is languished
and pale, pretend it's my father's
face and hell
if I know if he still uses hair product
anymore, he's bald.

Is this disease really about death,
or life? There is a dream
we've all had that we'd live forever,
that if we could, we might
try anything. I read
a lot, today I read we're *Generation
Immortality*. Spoiled?
Maybe.
We've got the best drugs
and the worst health
care in years.
But who cares? We may
live forever and never
even know it.

My mind reaches for the last line
of "Sailing to Byzantium"—
of what is past, or passing,
or to come? There's not a medication
made to say. But if it is immortality
we seek, time enough to reach
some indeterminate truth or simply to feed
our vanity, I won't forget to ask the gods
to include eternal youth.

I never saw myself
as a cricket.

America Is Waiting

It's like a long line of cars
and you're the only one on the road.
America is waiting.
Certainly you realize?
Immortality is the only thing
worth working for.
Come out and play.

It's a long, long line—

Claim your prize before you exit
the carnival is going up
in flames.

Choose Your Own Adventure

Or simply skip ahead,
skim the lines, unfurl
the binding, rearrange
your life in the order
you think best, whirling
forward and backward
forward and backward
again, again—pause
for a handmade illustration.
Pause for the prospect
of a repeat ending.
A prayer for apotheosis,
your narrow escape
in a slim existence.

Turn the page.

in communication, we trust

Halfway through the matinee, I

wake up watching a film to find myself
in the lead role. My eyes adjust from dark
to day, outside in the dim light on the street
where everyone is saying the same thing
differently. Between folds of paper and body sweat

and smoke from rubber or cigarettes, billboards
with all the ads defaced, hurried footsteps,
the glaze of morning, it occurs to me:
The whole world is a vast film set
in which props are continually shifting,
four extras reprising the roles of twenty-four characters

and people you've never seen before
playing your most beloved ones. Things no longer
run on lithium, only time. The roving camera
is a mirror where the lens's gaze belongs
to the audience, or else a recurring memory,
propped on stilts and a rotating series of images

displayed from an old Bell & Howell Cassette Projector
in which stutters may result in earthquakes. Narration dissolves
into a guided tour with no boundaries and hardly any pauses
for pictures or carefully planned detours, feelings
and ideas burst to the foreground with all the fanfare
of a very impressive PowerPoint presentation:

A word, a laugh, a look, some slight distress,
a passing thought or fear forgotten since childhood
like the ghosts that endure in homes, the dust
clinging to furniture throughout generations,
the memories that live on as ghosts,
the people and places you used to know, whispers or misheard

words, winding staircases that spiral
into an M.C. Escher painting, seemingly contained

but rather limitless. No end or absence
of surveillance in which someone, somewhere
is changing the frames, retaining an illusion
of motion for a single, vertiginous moment.

Death in the Digital Age

The night comes down
dark all day, over
the shoulder

in canted angles, surface
divisions plus or minus
a periodic voice-over

we flip the switch
and make a wish
to record

ourselves
recording
ourselves.

Simulacra

"The simulacrum is never that which conceals the truth—it is the truth which conceals that there is none. The simulacrum is true." —Ecclesiastes

Flip through the TV Guide
slow, meticulous, probing
as a Zen proverb's archer,
arrow, target—what
is on tonight? *Seinfeld, Friends,*
the Gulf War, or *The Awakening*—

was an Oprah book club special
at one time. Let's recite a few lines
from your favorite Greek tragedy,
or possibly *The Tragical History
of Dr. Faustus* (film adaptation).
I ought to heed the dangers

of selling my soul to Satan
in exchange for what?—
some fascination
with knowledge? No
I just want to live forever
in your arms—a line from

last night's *Melrose
Place*; they're all
the same. Let's kiss
passionate and do things
we wouldn't discuss
at the dinner table—

PARENTAL ADVISORY, EXPLICIT
CONTENT—and live in the flesh

content, while we're still able to,
before it's all wrinkled and loose
(you make a face and I do too).
Oh, let's wax philosophic, write sonnets

as time rushes to our backs
and moan tears of Cinemax
angst and pain (this is
just a dramatization)
before we bore and turn
the station.

Speaking in Tongues

Called in sick for this:
A tryst in the park
at midnight, Gramercy
Hotel high-rise, a sight
for scorned eyes.

Count the number
of drinks on the wall, count
the elegance of it all:
Ceilings sequenced entirely in light
bulbs, 24-karat lighters,

fine china plates
for show and carpets flown
in from China, and all
the passion of the boy and girl
exchanging I Love Yous

at the coat check
before their introduction,
before they've even met,
under the ambience setting
set at "passion fruit"—the usual

trappings of the fashion industry.
Me? I'm clad in plastic
armor armlets, a faux leather skirt,
Velcro ring around my neck
and seldom anything

else while guests walk by,
flash a shot and rub
my stomach, or themselves.

I spy women dressed as businessmen
and men that dress as women

more often than just this weekend, explaining
"Oh it'd be a sin not to take it
all in"—understand,
this is getting high society
happy. Down on the floor,

up in the clouds,
Calvin is crawling
among the skirts unfurled,
Calvin is crawling
and saying hi to every boy and girl.

The court's werewolves and witches
can't decide which to do first,
or where—they take turns
playing nurse with a needle
and watch the lines go by

as "St. Elmo's Fire" plays idly
somewhere. *We went searching*
through the wires
some squire screams
loud and lurid and giddy,

"It's Halloween, it's Halloween!"
Hollow hollow …
                    Hallowed be thy name
who has the keys
to this garden.

The fun just started.

Dear Chris,

Hey, what's up? I am writing this because Mrs. Peel assigned it. I am not really sure what to write, so I will start off by explaining my interests.

I like a whole lot of things. I like to play video games. I also like collecting comic books, and coins from all over the world (I think I am more rich in other countries than in my life here). I like all sports and my favorite teams are the New Jersey Nets, New York Mets, New Jersey Devils, New York Giants and the Anaheim Mighty Ducks, which some people call the Might Ducks of Anaheim. I play basketball, tennis, and soccer but there are some tough decisions ahead of me. I can't play all of them when I go to high school. Anyway, I have played for the Bergen Blackhawks soccer club for four and a half years. I really enjoy playing but mostly I like collecting the patches we exchange with other teams after each game. I love listening to music. My favorite bands are Guns N' Roses, Blink 182, and Ace of Base. My favorite hip-hop artists are The Roots, Defsquad (Keith Murray, Redman, and Erik Sermon), Nas, Master P and his brother, Silkk the Shocker. I don't know why musicians who make hip-hop are called artists and musicians who make rock are called bands but I could find out from my brother.

I have blond hair parted in the middle in a mushroom haircut right now. Everyone I know has a mushroom, except my dad. I always wonder if I am going to keep the same haircut when I go to high school. I always wanted short hair, but I'm always too afraid to make a change. It's too bad, because this long hair is annoying!

When I go to college, I want to do everything. Mostly, I want to major in Restaurant Management. My dream is to start a career by opening up my own restaurant and catering to everyone's pleasure. My mom might even be the chef, because she cooks the most delicious dinners and she learned a lot from my abuela.

I like the idea of making people smile and making money at the same time but my parents always say, 'if you don't improve your grades, you won't get anywhere.' I don't know why they want me to be a genius like my brother.

I like to learn about politics and geography and I can name a number of capitals off the top of my head. I also enjoy writing and reading books. My favorite subjects are English and History, which I think aren't really so different from each other. If I don't become a restaurant manager I would like to make it as a writer. I love writing because I like to record places and things from memories or my imagination.

This is the end of my letter so good-bye for now!

Your friend,
Chris

Endnotes for *Life*

An origin[i]

Sin[ii]

Condemnation[iii]

Sacrifice[iv]

Rituals[v]

Liberty[vi]

Yearning[vii]

End[viii]

Nothing[ix]

---

[i] Of fate or faith; "Don't turn around," she said. A mythology of

[ii] Or simply caution. Betrayal of an animal self, the underside of

[iii] So many grains of salt. My mother's advice at the age of 5 and what did I know of darkness?

[iv] Lot or Hades, tortuous roads, labyrinths, death,

[v] Of living, the waltz of life, any of these things? I was at the

[vi] Science Center for my next-door neighbor's birthday, left to my own devices, unhurried and released from vigilance

[vii] Only to eat cake. A hope, a sense, a want to see and be held or behold, looking sideways down the shaft like

[viii] Notes in passing, eyes clasped to see the very same thing.

[ix] Else remains besides the memory.

At noon, on a crowded city street

i.
The same way Madonna asked
"Who's that girl?" back in '87—
when I was what? Like three?
I want to know now. She's on the street
opposite me and if I stare long enough
she might actually see. Excuse me
do you have the time? No no no,
too trite, and why would I want to know
the time when I have a brand-new silver
Cartier with a special add-on neon light
my mother makes me wear. She cares.

ii.
Out on a crowded city street at noon
she spied him, amused, looking at her
as she looked at him, roaming past
the crowd then back again
to her eyes, to his smile (the whole while
people stared). The two
stepped closer and then shook
hands, "How do you do?"
he said. She said, "I'm Anne."
He grinned. Her Brooklyn accent brushed
past his skin, fumbled forward to his feet.
They walked toward the Hudson hand in hand,
at noon, on a crowded city street.

In the Dark Room

He snaps his flash persistent, pauses
for focus then gleams again, grazed
in a haze of impermanence
by which he spends his life
nostalgic for something

that had never been. He fears loneliness;
shadows elongated on the ceiling,
TV on only to hear the world
keep speaking. He meets
solitude on the street,

sees it in the fast cars
zigzagging past green
lights, the vast expanse of bodies
wading through seas of air waves,
day passing day, concrete longing.

It is never here,
suggested by the sharpie-stained
diner tray an old man raises
on the streets, hollering
wide-eyed as a present-

day Nostredame preaching
"The End is near"—
self-evident to anyone who owns
a watch or can simply tell
the time. Never mind

that we will all die
someday at the tick of a clock,
never mind that the Apocalypse

is all around us, incensed
in scriptures senseless

to the way the world works,
how we must be always waiting, forever
in anticipation toward
some inevitable unveiling.
Never mind

such life, or of living
in the moment,
the exact notion
of the passing
is never present—

it is not here.

Iterations

Midway upon the journey of our life
I found myself within a forest dark,
For the straightforward pathway had been lost.

Halfway between here and there,
I found myself arrested at customs
On suspicion of daydreaming.

Midway through Wednesday
I was aware that my watch, phone, laptop, microwave, alarm clock
Were all one day short and my life had been delayed indefinitely.

Entering the New Jersey Turnpike on bicycle,
I found myself regretting the luxury of car windows
And the ability to shut them, even halfway.

Halfway in a dream,
I realized I was actually awake
And in the dark had lost my way.

Midway upon my straightforward life,
I found myself in the dark
Within a journey without a path.

Mid-journey upon myself, in a forest, lost
And found—wayward in place
Of the straight path—a way of life.

Halfway in the dark, lurching forward,
I straightened myself upon the PATH;
A whole life lost between the journey's stops.

In a half-life, I dispersed uncertainty.

Half my life darkened between a path
Of leaves partly-parted to find I lost
All ways of journeying through time.
I stood still.

I lost myself in a straight life.
Midway and within the path.
Way of being forward, way of having
Been found in a dark forest.

In the middle of my life, I lost myself.
In the middle of my life, I found myself.
In the middle of the lost and found,
I lost my way and found you.

upon the
      within a
            for the
ability to daydream awake
entering wayward forward between
all   o n e   d a y
halfway through/midway in
the problem of starting anything
(luxury of regret)
I straightened myself
for rest
aware that I
was also you
any-body
a little death
a whole life lost
we find ourselves in the dark

When I am
Halved, I
Disintegrate

The Middle Ages (a meditation on memory)

i. Observations

I spent my middle ages carefree on the sand and shores of Miami Beach when I should have been in school, cutting everything except History, sleepwalking through class and exams, racing through hallways in various states; worn, sullen, suddenly ablaze (how a mood can change), surfing each morning, groaning with a new lover every Monday without the comfort of love. Taking everything in, sweat, salt, seashells speaking through the drift of generations, baitfish barely touching my feet in the shallow end, the morning joggers with their backs against the sun, forever pushing forward like some Hallmark postcard ... Making passes at my poetry teacher as I sat in class, rolling my tongue around my lips as she read something I would never read by Kerouac, on the road speeding headfirst, full-force ahead, stopping only to belt out a chorus, or a refrain, taking myself too seriously, or not seriously enough, slipping through the halls of my parents' home as a ghost, cruising along Calle Ocho or Ocean Drive in my father's silver '63 split-window Corvette, top down, shift up, blasting the Talking Heads, inwardly wondering what he would do if I took his car for little more than a joyride until I met him at a rest stop in Tennessee ... Falling in love with every girl that laid her eyes on me, writing poetry at lunch, between classes, during lectures on scraps of tissue paper and napkins, reading every moment I wasn't, imagining things that weren't really there ... Stealing my best friend's candy on multiple occasions—Gushers? AirHeads? Jolly Ranchers? All the flavors, particularly watermelon—Going to church every Saturday night instead of Sunday morning with my mother, never too early for salvation ... Writing the same love poem to four different girlfriends on four different Valentine's Days, coughing too loudly whenever I passed anyone I used to love, or who used to love me, no such medicine for lovesickness; recording all the memories I had, solely from the ways in which I wished the events occurred ... Throwing Ping-Pong balls into plastic cups balancing on railings, or cushions, or curbs, or my own two feet, kicking back, replacing sentiments with bland phrases, expressions I mistook for meanings ... Unofficially aging every April, hanging out at Coco Walk and Dolphin Mall, in smoke-filled bowling alleys and billiard halls, in swimming pools, in saunas, in Jacuzzis too hot to sweat, in decrepit arcades I thought I outgrew in elementary school or Junior High, in back alleys and dirt tracks, at weekend matinees, every movie conflated into only one long preview with no context or storyline, repeated without pauses one two three times as a frame imperceptibly clicked ... Head slung low in the back of Range Rovers and station wagons, in empty discos and dance halls, in dusty weight rooms that outlive their patrons, amid advertisements such as *Thirst Is Everything*, images of a Sprite can, gleam of sweat, an orangutan, basketball shorts worn inside out or simply reversible ... Never early or late, or rather only ever out of time refusing to look at clocks, watches, calendars, and the front page of the *Times*, or even mirrors (I only saw myself in passing), retrospective glances here and there about what I could have done or could be doing or would never do, or what would never be done by me or hardly anyone, parallel realities traced on parchment, each revision moving gradually through time and space, a lifetime of conjectures rooted in hypotheses ... In a void, imagining things that weren't really there, and would never be.

ii. Background and Research

My first assignment was five inches on a fire at the corner of Post and Leavenworth. (The Ledger was **cutting** corners.) **His** story, her story, my story, my-stery (That's **classified**). I interviewed five bystanders who gave me five different eye-witness accounts of what occurred. I later discovered one bystander was blind and despite last-minute over-the-phone conversations with his optometrist, spouse, next-of-kin that clarified one detail, more-or-less minor, my headline still read

FIRE DESTROYS

PROPERTY, MEMORIES

I tread on my dreams, **racing** a line in the sand with my foot to remind me that none of us lives straight **through** in the breeze. Feel it in each fingertip, a pinch of skin, the salt from each pore. Shake and disperse. I hurry throug**h**, **always without** from within, mis**taking** words for the things they mean instead of the things they seek, where they've been, intervening entry points into the w**hole** insoluble Mystery. Everybody asks. The same way everything **passes** ... **Taking** or taken or talking or tall king or tall kin or talcum. Come here. **Hall**ow. Hello. As**sociate ME**. Tathāgata, **candy** doves, body music, snare drums, flutes and liars from the halls of great civilizations, *Magdeburg Centuries*, ancient Byzantium, atrocity exhibitions, morose pop by Joy Division in the passenger seat of a car, as a passenger ... **Instead of** passé, give me *pasión*. **Cough**, laugh, gurgle, choke, sputter into something worth saying, choreograph our **medicine** dance. **All** of life relies on chance, arbitrary circumstance, what is in a word besides indication, that is to say *instinct*? What is in a word besides possibility? →

... **The memories** I have as a child, eyes agape in solicitous childhood, **of** five years and five months, or at nine, balloon mind, afraid of almost everything—*Junior!*—every converging train and each whistle and telephone ring and my mother's laugh and my dad's demands, and under tables all the faces I never knew from just their feet rising **high**er in the address of my dreams, **conflated** voices all talking separately at the same time around a dinner table, or at a cocktail party, or in my own mind, **into** and out of intuition ... Readjust the lens to find emptiness, which is **only** thirty-**three** frames per second, a vast expanse of **images**, the darkness of the cinema, the places my mind goes when I stop to think, an isthmus for hermetic memories lost **in** the **time** it takes for perceiving anything. **And time's passing** ... *Retrospective*ly *Illuminating the Dark Ages*, seventh edition vs. *The History Channel* **revision**: "600 years of degenerate, godless, inhuman behavior."

Record THIS. Or fast-forward the unpleasant bits.

iii. Methods

Cutting and pasting a collage from memories is a daunting task. Actual instructions are frivolous. I think it's pertinent to peruse experience in terms of scrapes and Band-Aids, a palimpsest, or arts and crafts. Pretend for a moment that it's bric-a-brac ransacked in an antique store, paved brick entrance to the mind, scoured for posterity or simply consigned to consumption; last, flimsy, like a Polaroid. And yet something is altogether lacking in a photograph ... Take video. Press play. The things I recall, I recall in zip pan, POV, a pullback shot without mise en scène. Or in darting moments, a brief flash, a passing scent, transposing and unblinking, and utterly distinct. Yet the whole of history favors similarities and slight anachronisms. How can this be? The schism of time is in a class all its own, and even now I am racing through hallways of my subconscious without taking notice of the hall itself. The lino. A railing. Reverse angles by which you see your own self speaking. Everyday details. Everything passes, although mistaking the halls of memory with a window into some other world is a deed done well. As a rule, I strive for lucidity in loneliness, long takes in cover shots, covering myself with the candy of imagination, the sweet gaze of the mind's eye that seeks amusement and finds instead the truth. It strikes without warning. I am either writing it down, or scurrying for a pen. And of course, my palm as paper never does the trick. Too many calluses, rough spots or swollen joints makes for disjointed prose, words rising and falling on the flesh, out of frame, a chronic fear like a cough, or coughing fits in an elevator filled with mysophobics without relief of medicine. Time is relentless. All the memories I have of a certain age arrive with an eye for dissolves and split screens, ellipsis narration, the Kodak Junior camcorder above me, rising higher, slung across somebody's shoulder. The older I got, the more conflated I became: rapid cuts into a montage set to something serious by Radiohead or Kurt Cobain's hoarse voice asking to be raped. Again and again. Only every five seconds, three more images arrive in the form of bridging shots: a birthday party, Carvel cake, wrapping paper unfolding a gown and tassel. In the interest of time, and patience, the camera skips the in-between phases, puberty, the middle ages, and suddenly time's up, or forever passing, the screen goes dim. Remove the reel and I don't exist, unfilled as an indecision, a figure shot from extreme distance, an unrequited gaze ... And the only retrospective bit I glean from this is to be wary of each revision. The second takes.

iv. Conclusion
Cutting history class.
Racing through hallways
without taking hall passes.
Taking Halls
as candy instead of cough medicine.
All the memories of Junior High conflated
into only three images in time
and time's passing.
Retrospective revision.

In Conversation

i.
"What is it
you wanted so badly
to tell me?
You seemed strange, especially
last night.
Love to know."

ii.
"No offense but
I think you are
missing
my sole
point to
the meeting, for your
information. I bear a cross."

iii.
"What I mean to say is
I will miss you.
Just
saying."

i.
"I had
enough
with words. Famished. I figured I love
delivery, quick and cheap, but all I really wanted
was to make
something real."

ii.
"A good defense:
a word that's already
in my mind and
always
being mindful of
skimming
the line."

iii.
"Speech is nothing
more than your lips
parting
farewell."

Living On Video

In 1990, I was five
and viewed my life
on VHS cassettes,

played God
for the first time
with fast forward

and rewind keys,
remote control
of memories, pieces played

back to me on a 24-inch
Sylvania screen;
we'd upgrade, of course,

to 36 and 48 years later,
a sparkling Toshiba
entertainment theater where we ate

TV dinners—reality
shows and soaps in the afternoon
on sick days

in my room; there's nothing
like wasting time
on someone else's life.

It wasn't my own
idea to buy a camcorder
for Christmas—that was Dad's—

and I was merely meant

to act in a medley of scenes—this is me
happy, this is me sad (wistful

eyes and a frown
that I had been practicing
my weekends around).

In Montevideo,
where white beaches sprawl
across the scene, uninterrupted

to interrupt our urban lives,
cityscapes and harsh demands
escaped by a stretch of sand,

there was the sound
of film rolling,
sudden. Stoic,

demure, I was
channeling some movie
star, Hollywood's

allure. Or it was me,
seemingly irritated, hand
in the cameraman's face,

playing paparazzi,
a quick chase to the car—olive Volvo,
not limousine—to live in secrecy.

In 2002, we traded timeshares
for a Carnival Cruise,
where there was tourism's

vulgar news on his shirt—

Same shit, different island
with repro on his mind. I land

in Rincon, I land
in Antigua, Haiti, Cancun, Canon
slung around my neck,

fanny pack and sun
glasses: this is me
on safari, this is me

nearby local
peddlers. I'm at the wedding
at St. Mark's cathedral,

reception at the Chateau,
video on YouTube.
Press *Play*.

Remain in Light

We broke bread and picked up the crumbs together,
sitting on a park bench
or in a diner booth
or at the dinner table,
re-heating all the leftover's
from last night's revelry,
the bits left in life after all the formalities.

Picnicking without nitpicking.
Steam rises and the heat goes on
with or without convection.
You and Me. And the inevitable yearning.
The way I want whatever's left,
like the half-life's gradual descent
into what? Decay. Nothingness.

Half a life spent looking
with too much certainty.
Uncovered and overdone,
and as staged as a casserole.
We remain in light, bare
boned and tight-lipped,
seen and not seen.

The great curve of our houses
in motion, born under
clutches, each turned inward,
crosseyed and painless
as in a prayer. As on a prairie.
Listening wind.
The heat goes on

once in a lifetime.
The heat goes on.

In communication, we trust

i.

In 1985 (when I was born) people spoke to other people,
across the street, over the fence,
in backyards, backs relaxed on loveseats,
"I love you"
sprawled out on the porch,
making love, or mourning; mornings
in the drive, bathrobe on, even
in suburban New Jersey.
People minded their manners,
but mostly their mannerisms, facial cues,
inflections, slight gestures and ticks,
seemingly visible to the naked eye.
These scenes are merely inventions.

ii.

At the dawn of the new millennium, people spoke on personal phones,
heads down, talking impersonally
through miles of unseen wires;
contact measured through bars,
not the kind in prison cells but cellular
devices, on the toilet, even
in cars. They traded in
rotaries for receivers and went
cordless. We're talking no strings
attached talk; no thing as bulky
as these beloved bricks.
People saw an exponential uptick
in forearm strength, exchanging
Russian novels with American slang,
half of which were never translated
intact. My girlfriend broke up with me
with mixed messages, mostly

emoticons, which I only grasped months later,
when the TV went missing.
People never asked what they had lost.

iii.
When I was one-and-nine, people spoke on earbuds or headsets,
but mostly it seemed like the voice was only in their heads.
People made friends on their mobiles,
navigating networks, poking other people through space
until their indexes atrophied
from inaction, free hands
directing traffic or simply jammed
in their pants pockets—
Michael Kors or Levi's—
updating their lives in real time.

iv.
When I reached a quarter-century, people spoke to their phones,
maybe even expressing intimacy.
They asked their smart phones
unintelligible questions like
"Is meatloaf one word or two?"
forgetting to specify
whether they meant the singer
or the food. They asked about the weather
or the quickest route to Kmart
and if they could really get to Quick
Chek in a minimum of nine minutes,
neglecting to mention the mileage
on the minivan, or anything
about the traffic on Route 17.
They routinely asked
about God and religion, conversions
from cubic centimeters to feet,
or about art, specifically

Cubism.

       My Cuban father communicates daily
with me, texting via speech recognition,
not recognizing that his phone, too,
hasn't learned his y's and j's.

You could say
we're not on speaking terms.

exchanges

wishing you were here
or having a great time
besides, always having
a great time on the back
of a postcard in cursive
scrawls, smudged
ink—everything seems small
when I look back at the past.

old letters saved, birthday cards,
holiday greetings, places I've been
a voice I only knew in childhood
wishing you were here
again, her hand inside
my hand, nothing so unchanging
as a signature, or a stamp.

the feeling of passing
(in transit)

In the taxi

I read Jane Fonda
Is Not Afraid To Die between
an advertisement for Fanta
Don't you wanna?

and another person lying
on the tracks; a woman
dead in Canal Street's
stop, and the start of spring

clanking through Bryant Park.
Don't you wanna?
Yellow, purple, red
gowns coming in again

on mute to hear the sound
of Riverside at fifty, maybe sixty
miles per hour. I see the scene
from the back seat:

the blur of bright white on blue
waves breaking on a broken
silhouette of silver shadows
that cuts a swath through

evening. Ripping wind.
Everything rises and descends
on foot, a break
————————

to pause for station identification
and then accelerate through
the minutes—the meter's ticking

measuring distance and time

and this moment, too,
opening up and unfolding
flowing through me
distance and time

and especially space
below and beyond me a puddle
reflects off the shimmering
sky and then dissolves

hands and head out the half-held
sliding translucence
and me, afraid to die,
or dying to live, dying

s l o w
so slowly, or sped up
scrolling down and through
at fifty, maybe sixty miles per hour

in the taxi.

The winter grazed him like footsteps

on porcelain, faint, or simply feigning,
barely touching, not quite, hardly even
there. He felt only the breeze
moving inside his jeans, whispered

silent as a gray hair, or wrinkled
skin, reminders of the time
forever passing, which could not
pass for him.
He cooled his heels at a housewarming

on Houston where people drank
Pimm's Cups, and dressed up
in collared shirts and black skirts
that looked more like the walls
colored over with fresh paint.

(Everyone was saying
the same things spoken
in different ways.)
He searched dark rooms in the Lower
East Side, and stood silent,

thinking about that one
line: *The heart gets bigger
as it dies.* So he inferred he must be
alive as something
from Lady Gaga beat louder and strangers

curved and twisted under smoke
clouds and strobe lights. He watched
the home in Greenpoint go dim
with abuse, or simply overuse,

everything rusted, or worn,

and he snuck forlorn glances
from the corner
of his eyes, a reflection
on mottled windows, recast
shadows, a face he didn't recognize.

(He could never go back again.)
He felt the season
as the unceasing hum
of a laptop breathing,
the dialogue of the people

he observed at bookshops
or chic cafés, their words
floating through him as so many Sunday
mornings; unsuspecting, like dust
in wind or daydreams.

There was only one
scene, and he felt
one moment
go on and on.
And on again.

In Silence

"Mind the gap," she said.
And to my left,
Caution
scrawled red
on a sign.
When I was nine, I collapsed

and only sprained my shin.
All I could say about the pain was,
"it
   felt
      like ..."
language collapsing

and now again
"mind the gap"
as someone recited
sol is not sole is not soul is not "mind
the gap" interfering,
persistent as a heartbeat, soluble. Never

mind divides in meaning.
Deliver us
from this inservice:
a life of missing the texture,
a life of just missing
each other,

contact measured in the friction,
bodies passing
bodies. This place is a dead zone
alive with sense and experience,
and everything in between

the ellipsis and the parentheses;

the meaning each mouth makes
in silence. Nothing
like killing time.
I was silent too when I heard
your words:
"Que saudade de você."

It was impossible to translate.
You never said what you meant,
or else meant what you said.
And then you left.
Instead I travel along avenues
through prolonged corridors

and bending stairwells
hitching and descending
past beatboxers and escalators
tides of confusion
rising and ebbing
murmurs like marbles

dropping on the floor.
Past hands clasping well-worn poles
samba here
bluegrass there
and everywhere, time's stains: remains
of newspapers and pamphlets

plastered to the ground
becoming the ground itself
now more black than white in places
now more graffiti than revelations
past psalms and static and hurry and noise
to hear her calm, articulate voice.

Stranger Who Was Passing

the end of a stroll	a hand resting on a door	children on a stoop	a mouth opening up
to a shout	brown leather boots	words on lips	hair entangled on a curb
the air before a breeze	rivulets of spit	rising dust	cinnamon
the sound of steps	on dead leaves	stranger who was passing	to witness

Stranger Who Was Passing

the end of a stroll   a hand resting on a door   children on a stoop   a mouth
opening up
to a shout   brown leather boots   words on lips   hair entangled on a curb
the air before a breeze   rivulets of spit   rising dust   cinnamon
the sound of steps   on dead leaves
stranger who was passing
to witness

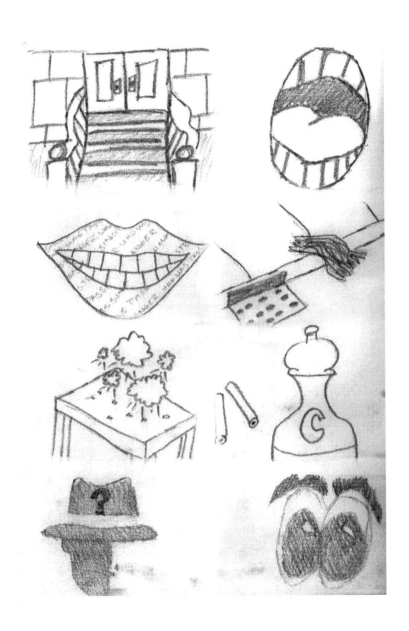

Stranger Who Was Passing

the end of a stroll
       a hand resting on a door
children on a stoop
       a mouth opening up
to a shout
       brown leather boots
words on lips
       hair entangled on a curb
the air before a breeze
       rivulets of spit
rising dust
       cinnamon
the sound of steps
       on dead leaves
stranger who was passing
       to witness

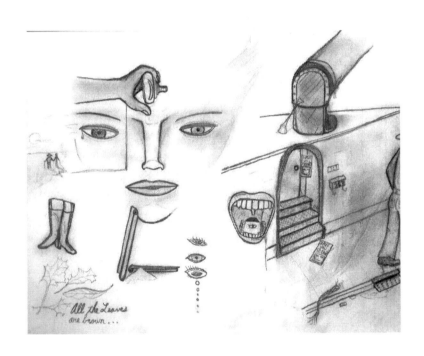

Forty faces, one line

huddled between the lot of them:
"... fears that I may cease to be" stopped on a dime,
sulking breaths of recycled air; women, children, men

of all shape and size—*mind the gap*—
cortege rumbles out, a new one rattles in;
stone faces, backpacks and briefcase claps,
a group of old men clothed in piss and gin—*mate, ain't no sin*—

guy holds young girl's hand in jealous taunts,
their concerns, different, the same;
she can't wait to grow up, he wants
to be nineteen again. The trend

is all cigarette grins and candy sneers amid the fart
of cold metal on hot gears, building speed
like a tea kettle, a slingshot in the dark,
hurtling through scenery unseen

till a jolt stills the whole place to a stop.
A polished old lady drops to her knees,
searching the ground; lino, unmopped,
while the roar picks up with a startling breeze,

purses everywhere, grocery bags and crying
babies; panic on such an April day.
A glance at the woman now, frazzled, unsmiling,
slipping back on her cushion as if to pray—

the whole ordeal quick and uncouth—
fumbling to put the dentures back in her mouth.

one under

lights dim
 platform hat in hand
voice to tell you
 where you are
(not where
 you've been)
slipping down
 the long slide
escalators and imitators
dylan here
 chopin there
outside 20
 and fair
a girl still
 more fair
shouting nonsense
 words whimpers
black heels
 clanking
when she takes
 her turn
"oh bollocks!—
 not another delay"
huddled in the rear
 of the train
"passenger action"
 "least 10 minutes"
bakerloo third time today

This that and the other

Like a prayer you will say to yourself
Like a prayer
Down on your knees
I like to do it on the typewriter
To feel the letters
To really feel them press
And depress, and press again—
And to hear it all happen, too,
This that and the other; this
Is the music that gets made
As I live my life
As my life is lived
This is the music.

A room, four walls, a song
To lose myself. A song.
Scotch taped boxes,
An empty valise.
The devastation of time.
My petrified smile.

I wanted to remember your voice, your mystery

your entire being, absolutely
everything, and the way
you closed your eyes and swayed
to a song
any given day
the smell of cinnamon
the bend of arms
in motion, or in serene
repose. A toast
to silence, to all of earth's

beautiful things—beautiful and ugly
and still beautiful—
all the breaths we don't see
to remember each love
and lovesickness,
to remember the ache
of wanting and how you forgot
what you wanted, or where you were
going, or who you wanted
to be, and how all of it
was a blessing.

I love the feeling of passing

trains as a passenger
on the train perched
with arms crossed and legs

dangling, branches in rhythm
to the beat: steel on steel,
stolen glances out the window
to meet bodies, faces, eyes

in transition, mouths moving
in a bad dub and then sudden
to a stop. In translation:
service delay. The smell of concern,

aluminum, deliverance, body
odors, hairspray, Head
& Shoulders, sweat and skin
and salt, preserved meat

packaged in a row, neat
or harried, limbs glued
to viscid poles in a cold
embrace. My eyes move

toward Plexiglas: a shard
of silver and similar figures
cut a swath through black,
halfway across the track.

ii.
I love the feeling of passing
bodies passing from the train
to the terminal. The G stops,

people and objects shake, props

rearrange in a momentary collapse
in the moments prior to
escape. Doors shudder,
exhale, and open as I wait,

impatient as ever, briefcases
and backpacks slap and arms
dangle by my side, briefly,
in the waning moments between

here and there. Click. Enter.
Exit. A body constantly
in transit. I pass cotton,
flesh, molecules; the space

outside us only vapor fabric,
a tempest of sweat and breath
and the barely-there
Queens air conflating with Brooklyn

air and now the smell of fried onions
and coffee in the carriage,
rising higher as people
make contact parenthetically.

iii.
I love the feeling of passing
head against the rattling
window when I close my eyes
or in disguise, half-concealed

in sunglasses not meant
for shade particularly
on hot days, June

or July, and then to blink,

like inklings of revelation
in the otherwise uncertainty
of going down, of being
under everything, over

and over again, slipping
down the long slide
of escalators and imitators,
caravan performers, opacity.

I come here to escape, to mind the gap
between the world of urgency and the dead
zone I sense when I see black,
utter nothingness attended in part

by the glare of advancing light.
A geometry of time whistles
in the distance as I sink deeper
in my seat, slouching toward eternity.

South to Savannah

The sun came through the dashboard and died
under another overpass, air as thick as dreams,
wanting as you might sometimes consider
just about everything: a crimson sunset
tapestry, hash browns and vanilla malts
and silver dollar pancakes, endless
notepads (a keepsake), a girl to kiss,
trackless beach, the whole world, or just to be
at least ONE YEAR OLDER. Unaware
(or reluctant to believe)
that you are the one telling the story,
subject and storyteller, soothsayer,
and say what you will
about twists and surprise endings
but in this version you're only ever
riding in the backseat
of a car, slipping down the long slide
of Carolina, south to Savannah,
weeping willows, watching
the people and places and things
as if they're only really
set pieces, silent until observed,
motionless
just like that double-slit experiment
you never knew
when the bell rang, when it came time
to turn all the papers in.

In a room with high windows

barely touching, not quite, hardly even
on mute to hear the sound
hitching and descending
to a shout, and say what you will.
The whole ordeal quick and uncouth
slipping down the long slide
any given day
down on your knees
under everything, over
and over again
in a room with high windows.

billboards

Scene 1, Item 1

The room was lit by her shoulder,
the angle of her chin and the nape
of her neck, and the way the sunlight
poured in, refracting and reflecting

off the dust, and the reflector,
the copper-color and polished edge,
and every finger and each figure
crouched clasping it from behind

and the umbrella propped in front,
and the props: all of them, each piece
of wood and draped sheet
and the cardboard's thin partition

shading steam behind the rack
of gowns, blouses, skirts,
folded fabric, the half-
hanged curtains and added effects,

extras, spare parts, accessories,
implacable shadows, the pores
of her skin, and the way her hands
glided when she raised them

to graze her hair, and the hair,
too, how it rustled in waves
unrolling toward a shore of certain
shouts, uncertain stage directions,

camera flashes, and the action
of memory, or the act
of remembering
all of it, and everything.

South of the Border

I walk by, seeing myself walk by
on a bag, someone's hand

gripping the paper handles
above my neck, my curved waist,

my gleam of sweat, me, half
a block away, and think,

you don't know self-fragmentation
until it's staring you in the face.

As the World Turns

i.
My head floated the way I feel
when I kneel
for too long before rising,

floated the way I feel
when I watch too much TV—
some scene

with a gun and two girls—probably
As the World Turns
that Mom left on

in neglect, or maybe to forget
the reason why she called us down,
just in case.

"Your abuela has died."
Except it wasn't like that
at all, it wasn't quick

and direct, words bounced
against walls, she said,
"she's in a better place now" instead.

ii.
Rest in pieces, or peaces, or appearances,
arrested ad infinitum—that's it,
or simply a wrest, singular,
a tool for tuning,
wrested pin by pin, turning
ever so slowly
into a stringed instrument
as a piano, or any machine,

some pianist's idea of melody,
and that's just it—there's no me
without any-body, specifically
you: a pair of eyes
is a you-topic vision, vis-à-vis.
I could not look at you.

I could not look at you who was not you
but an object in a box, not unlike the ones
I'm on, on and on, and on;
a loss, a gain, again, always
again, destroyed again
by the products of my own disintegration
and each of us objects
except you're incapable,
inside, or me on one side
and you on the other
(mankind in the middle)
unheimliche maneuvers
by which a man or woman
turns into manure
for some stranger's flowerpot, and to be
or not to be is not the question but life
is a run-on sentence, a series of comas
(semi-formalin affair)
or rather paragraphs without transitions,
two scripts passing in the night.

I couldn't look
because if I didn't look at you,
you weren't there, and if you weren't there,
you never died. And now I'm looking,
looking, taking my Me-ad in pieces
until I crack up, absinthe
of mon sherry, or any kind
of contact. I'm being

lengua frank, factual, actualizing
what it was I wanted to do:
Remember, remember, remember
Ana Esther Fuentes y Grave de Peralta.
That's you. Always with a broom:
La cucaracha, la cucaracha
y viendo telenovelas en su rocking chair.

I was watching too, rocking back and forth
in the foreground of this photograph
I framed inside of me, caught in the space
between the here-before and your hereafter.
I named my mother after you,
strictly speaking in fiction,
or rather speaking fictively.
You taught me poetry, breathed the music
into me, on my lips, my shaking fists
and buckled shins and my throat, too,
breathing, breathing
your own breath passed on to me
by your own death.
La música: that's my dowry.

I had a dream in which you spoke to me.
You asked whether I lived alone
and was I happy. Mixed construction—
I said genuine subject-verve relations
are only widdershins, and hear
I'm only whispering
a word to the wise, verbum sap.
When I am halved, I disintegrate.
Don't leave me, don't leave me, don't
please don't. Let me take this
with me, something to remember you by,
today through the by-and-by.
Good-bye.

New Balance

Blue and gray, and frayed,
balanced with new
laces sueded and laced
in ribbon: Twins in rubber
unmoving. Strange
for an object that makes
movement every day.
It's possible to imagine
the soles too.
Incapable without
a body
to inhabit.

Shot On Location

On the way to El Mirage we passed
the windmill farms, each fan turning almost
indiscernibly. I felt the wind come in
from canyons, a montage of
scorched earth, rust and fungus
clouds, rolling hills, *The Sun Never Sets*
On the Mighty, arid, shrill heat
of a California morning
rising higher when I stepped outside:
vista of a million Jeep commercials
in the drive-in of my mind.
There's Only One

Cut to white noise on the screen.
Cut to a man in the waiting room
accosting the maid who only came to clean
up the mess. Desert Princess.
67967 Vista Chino, Cathedral City. Cut
to some passerby's careless spit, the ice-scorched sand,
my saliva and sweat, the director's demands,
hands on hips, altering after every other
"How The West Was One"
—interruptions—
(my head in one place,
my body in quite another) ...

the Ferris wheel I rode all night,
one night in childhood, back flat to feel
the world move. And then I stopped too,
halfway there, halfway not,
paralyzed at the apex of the loop,
frozen in a half frown to hover,
helpless, above the ground where

we come around,

we come around,
we come around.

Palm Springs was a dream
I'd run along: long, wide streets, wide-
eyed awake and still longing
in the moments before sunrise:
Manicured lawns, espaliers, trestle-table patios, palm trees,
1950s swimming pools and the despair
of a million zigzagging fantasies
the moment they arrived
at El Mirador, or Araby Cove.

All of us and everything are born
in desperation and hope, and the swarm
of sightseeing captured in a magazine
for posterity, or for pleasure,
or for proof of something more.

Atrocity Exhibition

Flashes will fly across the sky, snapshots
of the whole scene, shrill voices will drown
out theatrical shouts and cries
while men with clipboards write
new stage directions and lines.
You will shudder slipping on words like ice,
returning home from paradise.

Chris Campanioni   meets   SOAPnet

This is me being		Title sequence: Hot
shot. Curt flashes unfurl		switch, cold open. When
on cue then stop.	*The moment*	the camera cuts to *Confusion*
A few dozen		all eyes gaze on
swarming eyes ensnare		the boy behind
the scene		the bar,
where silence seems		his gaze:
to wean in place of want.		far away,
Fingers snap		seeming to say
sudden like baby cries,	*(of) unrecognition*	I'M CONFUSED
interposing Pine Valley		instead of exuding
with the Upper West Side.		SOMETHING COOL.
Enter languid demands	*between*	The camera
and sanguine		moves from extras
assistants meant to act	*the eyes*	huddled at the top of stairs, or perched
as human fans, lest a gleam of sweat		on high stools
arises	*outside*	and zooms
on		to
an otherwise artificial guise.		his tank top,
Enter me, well-worn		speckled in bright jewels
in Levi's and a tank top		and queer
adorned		designs.
in sequins. My face		His mouth utters a few
rejoins in sequence with		languid lines while his face contorts in
every accented		wide-eyed
swoon and sway	*and the eye(s)*	smiles and
each voice	*on set*	sneers, a confabulation
instructs me		of misread signs
to convey.		and half-heard advice.
	is unsettling.	

The first kiss is a conflict

of subtle hints, secrets

secreting between eyes and chin,
and lower limbs—the hips,
the thighs, the knees, the twist
of my abdomen, a partial eclipse—
before saliva enters your unfurled lips.

The space between us
speaks in silence. Listen
with your flesh pressed
firm against my chest:
Neurons navigate
complex pathways,
coordinate movements
my limbic system meant
my corpus to convey. Logic did not

get us to this place. Outside
each muscle rises and contracts,
and reacts out of sequence
as my face lights up in sequins:
flushed damp and warm,
disoriented and re-oriented
at every turn. My self arrives
at self-consciousness
and my pelvis burns. A word

or phrase forms on my lips: *Sex sells.*
Sex cells. Neither notion works
well tonight. Fingers fumble,
falter, and fall unkind
on your wrist, behind

the wild motion of two bodies unbelieving:
They call it the nervous system for a reason.

Reconciliation

"Ya know, your body's like a machine,"
she said, big gleaming sips of green tea gulped
greedy, as if she had been swallowing air
instead. Me, bound in my chair,
reminded of Philomela except I have a choice,
"You don't take care of it and it's
like a car or anything else, it'll go."

The skeleton of my mother would know.

Strange to think of it that way,
your body and machines.
There is so much between
the two that doesn't seem
alike at all. I still recall
the first time I ate our garden's grapes,
the squirting sound my jawbone
made each time I chewed. I knew
they wouldn't last long—the grapes
and us—weathered by seasons and the cold
grip of something out of reach,
unbelieving. I meet in my
daily life a secret foreboding
of what's to come, of all that's passed. Believe—

our bodies were not made to last
our souls. The fall
in Brooklyn means Hel-
enium and breeze,
children racing through
the Hudson Promenade and everything
but salvation. Blame our scriptures, our books
that teach us nothing, and are nowhere

to teach us when we need to learn
to die. As flies to wanton boys are we to whomever
decides our fate. Debate is not required.
We are either damned or we are absolved.
There is no wrinkle in the fold
of stern faces and whispered prayers.

I can still see myself there,
kneeling, bound to my chair—
this one wooden and narrow, shelflike—
backaches and shadows
around me, incense in each answer,
heaving in the quiet and wondering
just what I should think now.

It is never how you pictured it would turn out.

Embodied

Back then, you could die
for it, now you just die—
Cavaliers, Puritans, all of us, I
find a delight in disorder
and the morbid thoughts
that plague our race,
our body's wild civility,

our soul's hallowed embrace:
Is what we are on earth
what we will be? Each time
I meet milk or honey, or the taste
of lips, I thank body and soul,
not concerned which one it is
that tastes, nor apt to separate

faith from what I know
is unknowable. There is no kiss
on cheek to calm us—merely enjoy
our reap from what we sow.
There are so many things in this world,
there are two things in this world—
my body, my soul—and after I grow

paltry, gray, and old, what
will I know? Body is a home
I live in until wrinkled, worn and die; what
endures of our lives?
There are only two things—
body and unbody that is in the person,
that is, no mahogany chair or curtain

in my mother's den—her favorite—

and what did she say when
she left this world and forgot the windows
which made her happy all those years?
Adieu. Those windows
staring back at you are gossamer,
and without panes to paint the pain

away from eyes that might just stare—
unthinking, colorless, eternally bare.

Before daylight, and after the black

of night has waltzed away,
leaving a silence and erratic crack

of cold and uncertain gray,
I wake, half drunk from dreams,
half anxious for day,

rising slowly like the steam
of a coffee mug that isn't there;
I never relied much on caffeine,

only bedtime stories and prayers,
and daydreams and made-up songs
when Mom wasn't there.

Holy words that right our wrongs are gone,
displaced with folks in suits that speak
with ease but talk in different tongues.

It's like this for 52 straight weeks,
with scores of crumpled pillow cases on satin bed sheets.

Soul

Affection. The effect,
postscript and/or
addendum, everything
written after the script has been
produced and performed
and in between adapted.
Characters behind curtains, no longer
personas. Persons. Everything
that's uncertain or certain
to be misconstrued as ideas
occluded by intentions.
The source of pain as a means
to please, certainly
everything pleasurable.
The mist after rain,
uninterrupted rainfall
on rooftops,
pitter-patter
intellect.
The thoughts I leave behind like footsteps.

Body

The footsteps.

Body + Soul

The sense of being.
A striving for a self
consciousness electrified by beauty.
The emblem,
the aim,
the end
of all finely-made,
well-loved
art, or else
a deed done well.
Love-making.
Always in love
with making
from an early age.
The shapes we make.
The weight of 21 grams +
the body
encasing almost everything.
The feeling of
embracing.

After the funeral

he woke and slept,
and thought of the contradictions
that he met in dreams,
fixations of being but not being
like seams unsown

in his mind.
Lines remembered
from Bashō:
Even in Kyoto
I long for Kyoto—unremembered
years ago, in the living

room after school, now
read incomplete, two lines,
two lives, the second between
the first and third
just missing.
It was like childhood

then, being here
and longing
for here, an oblong place
or time, elongated
and uneven in its signs,
its spaces—unreal, incomplete,

the spaces between the spaces
concealed not by air, but by not being
there, by nothing
that was something
in his mind. Reminded
again by the whole

dead procession—heads
in a perpetual state

of blank stares and unread
slates … he thought
of kissing, he thought of sex, the birds
and the beats

he used to make
with his mouth
in the waiting room,
any waiting room
when he was bored
of waiting because the end

almost never came
until it did. He thought
of shapes rising,
convex realizing concave,
trite sayings
in dust, littered in wind,

recalled half-drunk, or dazed
in passing, all requiems,
one life to leave, anything
but the funeral,
people talking suddenly,
without warning, funereal

speak, synonyms
for heaven and God—
"she's in a better
place now"—and still
seek the measure
of uncertainty,

of being and not being,
of an aunt who wasn't
an aunt who died
(and yet didn't)
and her nephew who wasn't
and survived.

The imagined screenplay from a real-life romance
(with liner notes)

Obligatory Introduction
*The first scene
is always a hint or glance: perhaps
a panorama of New York City opening
on the banks of the Hudson, sun
peaking at dawn like a Hallmark
greeting card, merely an intimation.
Or else an invitation
toward the future, flash
forward, a kiss without context
so that when you come back,
nothing looks exactly
as it first appeared.
How did we get here?*

i.
Summer again.
These days it's a whirlwind.
Better than a wasteland
(A swirl of graffiti on West End
and 69th Street, three blocks
from ABC) Do the math:
frantic crowds, panting mommies
and slack-jawed fans. I don't stand a chance.
They're in awe. All lined up in a shooting gallery,
a pattern with no origin in a room meant for *The View.*
Heads nod,
      skirts unfurl in the wind,
            cameras flash on cue.
My script doesn't include anything prior to
Scene 1, Item 1: *All My Children*
screaming—"ice cream!" I freeze
each time I walk past,
just a moment
every morning, abrupt as an ambulance

wailing down West Side Highway
in an otherwise somnambulant waltz,
eyes half-closed, half dreaming.
Weekend At Bernie's this isn't;
not dead yet
and this ain't no paradise.

Inevitable Conflict
This act is all about not acting.
Characterized indecision. Character exposition
through trite conversation or else explained with symbolism:
Boy stands at the vending machine for more than sixteen minutes ...

ii.
Despair, ennui, heartache. Sometimes
even misery. They streamline the whole range of human emotions
for 50-second
commercial breaks. I went to school to write, not rehearse.
Now it's a high-wire act, suspended
in mid-air
five days a week, syndicated and syncopated
in fifteen different languages
and captions for the hearing impaired:
Trite proclamations and pained looks
of consternation or constipation depending
on the attitude or what the script calls for.
I exude confidence on set,
unsettled in private, tortured
between lurid storylines and my own
naïve dreams. Somehow I stumbled into daytime
TV; the extra man, the under-5 over-the-top
Cabana Boy, forever
shirtless, occasionally
oiled up, gleaming in the glare of the HD lens:
One Life To Live
TAKE TWO
          TAKE THREE
(it's difficult to excuse the irony)

We come to the climax—
or a series of climaxes
if you are seriously counting—
enacted to give the audience some pay
off, or catharsis, and at the very least,
their money's worth. The scheme
usually implemented is "a do or die" situation
where doors of escape for either or both
of the two characters go on closing,
one by one, leaving them with only a thin chance
that demands display of their best qualities.
This results in a so-called
jaw-dropping, breath-taking, arm-grabbing
moment for the audience. Incidentally,
this framework cannot be applied to all stories.
Some genres demand a more delicate handling:
Chocolate or flowers?

iii.
Summer again.
Too hot to sweat, either in decrepit bowling alleys, Lucky
Strike Lanes, or else daytrips to Belmar to break
monotony. Always
moving but hardly moving. Automated
reply, returned to sender. A life like
sitting ducks, waiting
for something that never comes.
Everything rendered hopeless.
Everything but the girl—
not the band,
just her—
salvation in a smile.
                    Twelve months later ...
We race from Brooklyn to Queens like leads
in a Mamet thriller, real
or imagined, hand in hand,
bouncing through boroughs like two pockets full of change.
I'll never be the same.
We break into Bloomingdale's—

the big one on Broadway—and rearrange
everything, mix up
electronics with undergarments
so people can really wear their BlackBerries to bed
(that part is pretend).
We eat our way through Chinatown,
Greenpoint, Astoria, a stew of love
consumed ravenous, broth thick as our thighs.
We live so fast, we travel in time. She's early
as my Christmas present. Gift-
wrapped, bow-tied, Heaven-sent. Invented
in Korea, assembled in Brooklyn,
US: A year in the making.

Still Life

Silence to say
I lost you repeating
On airless days turned

Inward on a track
Background of reflections
In the fountain of a park

Flower petals
Wooden benches
Breeze stirring slightly

Occupied parking space
Vacated lots, faces lost in passing—
We pass every day

Smile politely sometimes
Say a few words something
Casual, neutral, nice

As a swimming pool in June
Ice cream at midnight
Coffee in the cold

Picture in a magazine

Locker Room Talk

"She said it tasted like sun-kissed saltwater
from the Caribbean Sea." I nodded slowly
and pulled my tank top down my back.
"And do you believe she actually said all that?"

You said this as we were leaving the locker room
talk and moving through body language,
muscles and machines, and the sea
of bodies and the smell of metal

and rust, and the touch
of cold steel and the soft, padded bench,
and the way it feels
to rip ligaments and tendons, limbs

extending, each sound drowned out
in the gymnasium. The way it feels.
Chiseled and diminished. Stippled
in the perimeter of each looking glass.

The way it feels. You asked me
how to do it right; you
asked me what part this worked.
"Torso," I said. And the toe bone

connected to the foot bone
foot bone connected to the leg bone
leg bone connected to the knee bone ...
I sang the song I memorized in grammar school,

sweating and sighing
in between repetitions
of rope twisting

I wondered if you caught the religious reference

and gradually, more people and places
emerged from the locker room.
"I met her on Craigslist," you said.
Missed connections:

You were the serious man with the briefcase and cardigan
Staring into space on the F train
I was your temptress. Devil in a blue dress.
I wondered if you caught the film reference.

"We were seeking affection," you said.
I imagined the scene:
baking pear tarts in convection ovens,
exchanging clothing, and other woven

accessories, scarce handkerchiefs,
soft and padded, and the pashmina shawls
that she would wear
around her hips, mostly

when they went dancing. You added,
"Girl really put her back into it,"
panting in reflexive benedictions,
a puddle on the floor. You added,

"Girl really made me sweat."

Billboards

i.

It's strange when everyone you know is on a billboard. And when everyone knows you by your billboard. *Look, that's Park Avenue and 49th Street* and when you pass yourself on the 6 train, it's unsettling. Everyone you meet at work is built like that: sun-tanned, smooth skin, 6 percent body fat, jagged lines tattooed down the middle of a torso, laid out as a playbill. Categorized, categorically circulated, billed in bulk: 20-26, Hispanic and/or Caucasian, can do accents, dirty blond, hazel, athletic, flexible, 6 feet and above all else replaceable, swapped out at the snap of someone's index finger when he or she was really looking for a blond or brunet, but nothing in between; it means being on hold. Seen through split-seconds and shuttered eyes, or in disguise, constantly balancing between self-love and loathing to rise and fall as billows, broke for 6 months until the residual check arrives, or a phone call places you in Hong Kong or Rio or the Czech Republic, as phone calls often do, to occupy your vacancy. It's as strange as the photographer's request to *Be Natural*, or when the crew demands a smile as you tremble and crunch below an artificial waterfall, weary and cold. You booked BlackBerry when the casting called for black, dreadlocks, and in parentheses (urban); it's strange when you can be all of these. I've never been good at choosing.

ii.

A woman in satin chooses what's *IN*,
smiling when she thinks nobody is
looking. Months later, the workers transcribe
the good stuff on animal flesh and leave the rest

for peddlers to hawk around Times Square.
Upstairs, I'm dressed, strapped down and suffocated
in layers, lambskin, rabbit fur, synthetic
leather, every shade of suede, strange

hands in my hair—immoveable
from too much Animalistic—perched

on a cushioned chair, four legs
to balance my two. On the street,

everyone is mesmerized by shoes.
High-heels, loafers, slip-ons, chanclas,
moccasins, slingbacks, ballet flats,
espadrilles, plastic Velcro sneakers

with an orb on the tongue's tip,
flickering faintly, extinguished.
No one's ever seen that before
and just to make sure it won't happen

again, the sign says NO PHOTOGRAPHY
ALLOWED. Meanwhile, a man coughs
on my neck. Something sticks. I haven't felt
that kind of contact in months,

and when hair and makeup is done,
I see a stranger staring in the mirror,
absently. Routine motions fail
with pins and needles, some seamstress's

idea of overstitching, and the feel
of barely-there, not-quite, almost,
not-right, falling through
fingers and easily forgotten

until gone, begins to enter me.
Whose dream is this? I sleepwalk
through flits of nostalgia and romance,
wanting and waltzing with a day-

drunk's lethargy, or anyone
who knows anything about leisure.
I can't seem to hear anymore.

People's mouths move in slow-motion

and sound dulls—it must be jet lag,
soul catching up to body, the hallowed
delay. I squint and pinch my arms.
I try to recall details. I keep notes.

I'm not lonely, if that's what it seems
like, always writing things down.
I am also somebody's lover, somebody's son.
And yet, I feel abandoned.

Rite of Passage

I have been a word in a book.
I have been haunted
by history, the pangs
of the past. I have been
dreaming. Arrive at the moment
of my life. Arrive to know
you knew me; you were here.

epi-logs

I'm walking down Bowery in the middle of January, five degrees, thermal running pants on—you know the kind—nothing left to the imagination, but five degrees, mind you, given the wind chill. Mind you.

And I can see the woman approaching, I can see her gaze, I can see where she's looking, face down, step-by-step. And I normally wouldn't mind—really. I wouldn't normally mind so much.

You can get used to anything.

This woman is in her fifties; she's wrapped in fur, she's got her snow boots on and a scarf and she's talking on her cell phone but her face is down and her eyes are stuck securely on my crotch. She doesn't even pretend. Maybe after fifty we stop pretending.

Every person is a beautiful being; we were meant to be sexual. We were meant to enjoy all our faculties … and people will say I set myself up for it. People already say all the time: hey, why are you complaining? You're an UNDERWEAR model, what'd you expect? You've asked for it.

So use me for my body, that gives you permission. That gives the whole world—this lady included—permission. Use me for my body. But please—

Use me for my mind, too.

***

Idea: A story that follows the seasons of the year at various points of each character's lifetime.

Spring → Summer → Fall → Winter → Out of Season?

Illusion of constant change, implicit processes of cultural production, polyphonic narrative, devastation of time. Fashion as a verb. Et cetera.

With photos?

***

Through the haze of dark and oblong glow of strobe lights and disco balls, I spied you, sighing in the corner, couple of martinis in but bored and slightly abhorred by the Madonna gyrating within the walls—it was Eighties Night—and when our eyes met I turned my head. We walked forward; we passed each *other. We were both aware of being in the presence of the other. The games we play. Each of us aware. There was a moment I could have looked at you again, in the eyes, with you looking at me at the same time. It passed too.*

***

A student of mine says he's trying to be a writer.

Trying? I say. What do you mean, trying? You write. You are a writer.

The biggest obstacles in life—for those fortunate to live in liberty—are the ones we create. How can you ever do anything if you don't even allow yourself to recognize you for who you are, for what you do?

And then, on the long drive home, I think about how little has changed. You get published, you do book signings, you lead panel discussions, you instruct. You still have all the same self-doubts. You still feel like the loneliest person in the world (sometimes). And you use your solitude, all of it ...

Nothing really ever changes anyway.

***

I wanted to encapsulate everything, or as much as I could remember, as much as I could feel to know it was real, because it had to be real if it was to be written: the exhilaration and optimism, the failure, the abject fear of falling or even standing still, for just a moment, the panic of being alone or unwanted or discarded or unwatched, unnoticed, like standing at a party and not knowing any of the guests, North American arrogance, the shame and embarrassment, characteristic vulnerability, the utter ignorance, the joy of discovery, the euphoria of learning, the awe and wonder and knowing it as only temporary, tenuous reluctance, insecurities of being, the horror of knowing, the fake laughs and smiles and the face you put on (maybe the one you forgot to take off) for the public, for anyone you never thought you could bare yourself to, how you could look in the mirror and hate yourself, so simply, the devastation and agony, the fact of seeing, and seeking, naked lust, animal habits, forlorn silence, fever of release, the searing pace and hurry and calm, the boredom, dead days, endless days, the days that are passing or already past, one by one, gone to the gallows, the patient resignation (doomed but undefeated), the terror and desperation and rage, the feigned confidence, the promises and possibility, the impossibility of growing up.

***

"I do not know which to prefer,/The beauty of inflections/Or the beauty of innuendoes,/The blackbird whistling/Or just after"—*something*

Clarence would say, only in public, maybe at dinner. Purposefully enigmatic.
Et cetera.

***

I turn on music, usually something by New Order, Talking Heads, Purity
Ring, A Certain Ratio, Cold Cave, Cut Copy—something catchy, something
that will shake me out of my slumber like a sweet surprise. I put on a track and
I write until it stops. A new track comes on, I shift everything: the tone, the
scene, whatever images flood my mind, even the lyrics themselves, music
bleeding across the page, slipping in and out like static on an old TV.

***

I wanted to become anyone, so long as I was not myself.

***

We came up from the face down.
Cheeks, lips, especially the jaw. Traceable to fish. Fish face. No surprise
there, really. Capture and consumption. Mate acquisition. Quite a catch; a
fish out of water. No surprise at all.
From the face down.

***

And because I feel, in my own way, if I don't write, then I never existed.

***

I see the poem as a shutter roll of film being played out in pieces on the
reader's VDT. Which movie does he or she see?

***

The thing I love about poetry—I mean, besides everything else—the part
of poetry which will always distinguish it from every other piece of writing is
the mystery.
The mystery: the enigma of a single poem and a single line of a poem, and
a single word of a line of a …
Comes from the creative stimulus, which is to not know what it is you are
writing, even after you are finished writing it.

***

I hear everything. I have my ear to the ground. Left and right. I turn over.
Right and left. I hear everything. The swiftest sound.

A page turning.

***

For over half a century, Fidel Castro has destroyed Cuba. He has ruined the lives of the persons he calls his people. On the island; outside of the island. Generations of Cuban emigrants live in a permanent state of exile. Generations of Cubans emigrants refuse to return, so long as he is breathing.
We collectively wait.

***

Because there is no goal except to create sounds and from sounds to create rhythm. And from rhythm to create meaning. But the spaces between the first and the last are boundless.

***

Critics want to talk about plot, about sequence, about characters. But the only element that interests me in my work is the reader. I write for a communication, between myself and anyone reading.
You can't fake it. You can't fake a thing like that.

***

My mother is sitting in the kitchen, reading. Re-reading. "Yeah, no, you write very well. I wanted to tell you, the way you use language, you know, is beautiful, the words move like I'm watching a movie down the page, you know, like a film, but I could have done without all that sex. I could have done without Brazil."

***

"How does pubic hair end up there, on the inner curve of a urinal?"— *something Clarence would say, maybe out loud.*

***

But then I read about these vacations, these "expeditions," and I wonder if Castro's approaching expiration has already opened up the island to something even worse: the promise of "educational exchanges" like the ten-day journey Abercrombie & Kent Cuba has been taking reservations for since 2013.

What is the fate of Cuba? Always to exist in a state of oppression, pimped out and then betrayed, and again, sold off to the highest bidder: a herd of tourists with nothing better to do than to "ensure their daiquiris and ropa vieja are up to par. ... Steam-training across the island."[x]

---

[x] From an UrbanDaddy advertisement for Abercrombie & Kent (July 28, 2013).

What is the fate of Cuba?
Betrayed by anyone looking to make a buck.
✳✳✳

What could be more utopic than writing? The possibilities that exist on a
blank page ...
✳✳✳

RealClear Politics tweeted that I was creating the template for the modern
author. The Brooklyn Eagle asked their readers if I was the most interesting
man in the world. Sometimes you feel like you're living in a short story. And
it's written by Borges.
✳✳✳

But I don't want to tell you what's outside of me. I don't want to tell you
any of those things ...
✳✳✳

He Googled photos of Corey Haim, the whole way home, to feel better
about himself.—*something Johnny Baker would do, maybe habitually.*
✳✳✳

I still don't know if she meant the country, or the third act.
✳✳✳

Several readers asked me why I didn't write a memoir. Well, here we are.
✳✳✳

Idea: a story that's told in letters (epistolary and the alphabet).
There is a desire to move from the cinematic to the photographic; I mean
to focus the writing on a single object/subject/snapshot, which could, perhaps,
produce a more beautiful picture.
✳✳✳

I would regret my entire life; I would want to live it over again.
✳✳✳

I never was very good at acting. I never was very good at playing the role.
Because the true pretending can only come off in our genuine awareness of the
real. Only those of us with the most secure grasp on the real can pretend; can
really be good at the performance.
And of course I didn't know what was real; I only knew the camera was
always on.

***

Literature sustains life because it captures death in its forward march. Clickety-clickety-clack, the wheels go round and round …

***

Each time I re-read something I've written, I learn more about it (and maybe, also, myself).

***

There are times of arresting melancholy.

I don't know what I'm writing. I don't know whom I'm writing for. I mean readers. It's like that Brian Eno song: "No One Receiving." Is anyone on the other end? Is anyone there?

***

Each time I re-read something I've written, I can transport myself back into at least two separate occasions: the moment I was writing it; the moment about which I was writing.

It's like loving in a different language.

***

It would be closer to a photo album with fixed instances and incomplete figures: offer the reader to trace it by permitting *the gaps.*

But first I need to go; I need to see Santiago for myself.

***

Several people discuss the moment they were near-death: an image of an entire life flashing before them. I had mine when I was born, but what could I have possibly seen?

***

I didn't want to write words, I wanted to make music with words. I wanted the words to jump off the page. I wanted the reader to immediately re-read the paragraph they'd just read—not because he or she was lost, but because they were so INSIDE the prose. In that way, I could re-create the experience for anyone who wished to contribute: the obsession … the joy and euphoria and uncertainty of creation.

***

Idea: re-write Talking Head's "Remain in Light" (a poem that follows each song from the record?)

***

Can you hear my voice when you read the order of the words? … All in the arrangement … and everything and all of it is only a matter of listening.

Whose voice do you hear?

***

All this writing suffers from the same old shit.

***

Everywhere and always is the endless stream of seats unsat, metaphors to match the space vacated by your leaving.

***

Even this *moment will become another story. Momentarily …*

***

The book has pretensions of playing with literature, and at the same time establishing a relationship between writing and metaphysics, of clarifying the point: there is no such thing as memoir; all writing is memoir. Of initiating the game and inviting the reader to participate.

***

All writers desire an audience, or else we'd be writing diaries. But even those are meant for someone else.

It doesn't surprise me why I started working as a model; why I continued working. The two professions require the same act of self-immolation: Bare yourself, dissolve yourself. At the same time. And you have to be willing to do both. You have to be willing to recede into the ether at the very moment you reveal your soul.

***

I wanted to play that game, making marks at the level of linguistic disintegration, the division of language into all its various components, even on the sonic level, even on the level of interruptions and unintended meanings; I mean mistranslations.

I mean mispronounced revelations.

***

Before I go on trips, I write out instructions. Meticulously detailed, down to the digits, sometimes in bullet-points. In case I die.

Give her Fashion, *give her* In Conversation *(clearly). Hell, give her the*

Tourist Trap *manuscript from 2007.*[xi] *Madeleine will know what to do. Madeleine will work it out. She could squeeze out gold dust from dog shit.*

An almanac of me to you.

I think every writer does this. And sometimes, it isn't just long trips, it isn't just being up in the air. I'm leaving the house today. I'm going underground. The world is a dangerous place. Death is in every step we take, and especially the ones we don't.

Death, you know, is everywhere.

***

The author-as-a-brand affair is exhausting. I'm keeled over my laptop, at this very moment. Really.

I say different things to different people and the articles all read strikingly similar. "He wears many hats." For the record, I hardly ever wear hats, not even a Mets cap at Citi Field, not even a beanie when it's snowing. "He wears many hats."

People will write whatever it is they want to write about anyway—no matter what you tell them—the script has already been produced and performed, and in between adapted, remember?

***

It's a terrible feeling. It's the worst feeling in the world. Like your whole life's been boiled down and there ain't nothin' on the bottom of the pot.

***

I love engaging in the discussions, I just don't like all the things I have to do for the privilege of the opportunity. All the endless promoting. Shouting to the heavens. Enclosed is a copy of … A story about media and communication … The intersection between Manhattan and Latin America … Recently selected as one of the … If you'd like more information …

The template is broken.

***

Everything is memoir and everything is also elegy. We don't dream so that we may forget—we dream so that we may remember. And to remember is to recapture—to try to recapture. What's going or gone. What's already slipped through our fingertips.

[xi] Read it in any order you'd like.

***

The goal is not to live life but to live life as poetry and vice versa, to make every moment count and to count the beat of it: that rhythm that is life and becomes life until everything is beautiful, inherently and undeniably, because there's no other option. Because there's no other way of looking at the world.

***

Recurring dreams of revolving doors; of being stuck inside.

***

And I even invite you to look.

***

I'd like to take my name off all my future works. Because it's about the work, not the writer. The writer re-directs everything, obscures everything.

What can I say about anything involving the work that could better express what I've already written? Everything is in there. And especially the parts I still don't understand.

***

To see what I can never see—will never see—because I am unable to get outside myself: the outside and the inside and the in between; the reality and its veneer.

***

It's not just me. I think everyone privately thinks about death. I think there are many things that people keep private, things that people never utter, things that people hold deep inside of themselves, even to the last breath.

***

To own beauty is the first lie of it.

***

And I even invite you to look.

***

My mother's sitting in the kitchen, reading. Re-reading. "And why did you have to mention the way I like to read? Family moments, our accents, the red Doberman squatting—Amy would not have been pleased, okay— yeah, no, the paper, too, and ABC … c'mon, Christopher, you know; I mean, c'mon, REALLY. You know, you're gonna get into trouble. You're not supposed to share these things. And you killed Ana—how could you have killed off Ana? You're too much sometimes, you know. You go too far.

You never know when to stop."

—Oradell, March 12, 2014

ACKNOWLEDGEMENTS

Grateful acknowledgement is made to the editors of the following magazines, journals, and anthologies where the poems here first appeared: Fjords Review; theNewerYork; Vending Machine Press; Squawk Back; Across the Margin; Red Savina Review; Control Literary Magazine; Literary Orphans; Rosebud Magazine; the Williams Writing Prize (2005, 2006, 2007); the Academy of American Poets Prize (2013); and Amaranth. John Campanioni illustrated "Stranger Who Was Passing" on pages 100 and 101; Antonio S. Galica re-translated the poem into the collage pictured on page 103.

For the last half-century, poetry has been on the backburner instead of being at the forefront. In American culture and elsewhere, this is the pattern. There are so many great teachers, readers, and writers who are actively altering this arrangement. I had written that nothing is more utopic than writing. And poetry is the ultimate expression of utopia. Nothing is more dangerous to all forms of dictatorship. In poetry, we endeavor to do the impossible. We endeavor to make the world stop spinning. But the endeavoring is all that matters. The possibility is all that matters.

Poetry lives.

And it will always live, because poetry lives inside each of us.

3.23.2014

Chris Campanioni fell in love with poetry at nine years old, when he wrote a poem to his abuela, Ana Esther Fuentes, after she passed away. Since then, his work has appeared in the Star-Ledger, San Francisco Chronicle, Bergen Record, Herald News, The Brooklyn Rail, Fjords Review, theNewerYork, Quiddity International Literary Journal, Vending Machine Press, Squawk Back, Across the Margin, Amaranth, Control Literary Magazine, Red Savina Review, Literary Orphans, Lime Hawk Literary Arts Collective, and several anthologies, including the 2013 Academy of American Poets Prize and La Pluma y La Tinta. He is the author of two novels: *Going Down* and *Fashion of the seasons*. Find him in space here: www.chriscampanioni.com

Made in the USA
San Bernardino, CA
02 March 2015